The Seductress Trap

Jac Sherry

About the Author

Jac Sherry lives and works in Madison, Wisconsin where she shares a home with her lovely wife and a very nice cat.

Jac explored writing in the 1990's when she posted some stories to fanfiction sites. She even won multiple awards from the Wisconsin Screenwriters Forum at the time. Then life got in the way with a career, a house and family. Twenty-five years later life has begun moving out of the way and Jac can write again.

Supercharged by the isolation of the pandemic lockdown, Jac was able to write her first novel, *The Seductress Trap*, in about five months. She now has a pile of other stories she wants to write and is hoping to publish more soon.

At her day job Jac spends her days buried in numbers, spreadsheets, and databases where she feels perfectly comfortable. In her spare time she likes to bike, paint, play the ukulele or go birding. Any additional time Jac can find she spends with her wife, with whom Jac is still giddy in love despite the passing years.

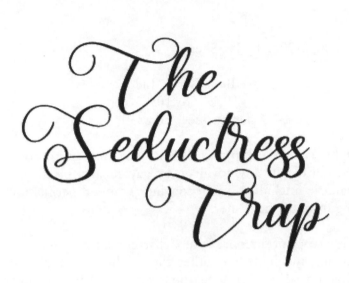

The Seductress Trap

Jac Sherry

BELLA
BOOKS
2022

Bella Books, Inc.
P.O. Box 10543
Tallahassee, FL 32302

Printed in the United States of America on acid-free paper.

First Edition - 2022

Editor: Medora MacDougall
Cover Designer: Heather Honeywell

ISBN: 978-1-64247-336-0

Dedicated to my lovely wife. With you I am
greater than once I was.

CHAPTER ONE

"Heeeey, ladies!"

A pounding musical beat boomed through the dark space filled with people. The room was damp from sweat and spilled drinks. The smells of stale beer and faint vomit permeated the heat. A male voice interrupted over the house speakers again. "Are you ready to parrr-tay?"

"Woo!" came the resounding chorus of women and gay men in the crowd.

Angel Lux sat at the bar with a drink. She ran a thumb through the condensation dripping down the side of her glass, wetting her fingertips. Behind the bar glass shelves were stacked with multicolored liquor bottles of all shapes and sizes. Behind those was a bar-length mirror that deceptively doubled the inventory. She glanced past the bottles to eye the action on the reflected stage. Disco lights kaleidoscoped through the liquors and bounced into her eyes. She squinted and looked away.

"I didn't hear you!" teased the emcee.

"Woooo!" the rowdy mob cheered, more enthusiastic than before.

Angel glanced at the mirror again, catching sight of a stray curl on the side of her head. She reached up and ran a hand past her ear to slick it back down with the rest. She took another drink and tidied her muted lipstick by trailing her fingernail along the edge of her bottom lip.

A tall drag queen with an enormous blue beehive wig buzzed behind the bar. She stepped over to wipe up the ring where Angel's glass had been. The bourbon over ice in her hand, Angel lazily turned to face the stage and examine the crowd more closely.

The usual throng of gay men, the regulars, filled the left side of the dance floor in front of the stage. It was the right side of the floor, packed with carousing cashiers, college coeds, administrative assistants, professional women, and even a few housewives, that held her interest. Angel surveyed that crowd like a lioness studying a herd of gazelles on the savanna, sizing up one woman, then moving on to the next and the next. She had been watching and waiting for a while, and a few prospects had made themselves apparent.

The emcee cranked up the music even louder and the entire building began to thump. "Looks like this house needs some work done. Good thing somebody showed up to take care of that. How would you ladies and gentlemen like to party with…" The emcee paused for dramatic effect. "…the Handyman?"

The audience hooted in reply.

Angel watched as a fine, well-oiled specimen of a human male strode out from the left stage wing, his thumbs hooked in a leather tool belt mounted over extremely tight blue jeans that threatened to tear spontaneously at the breakaway seams.

"Because the Handyman loves to party!"

The crowd cheered, grabbed dollar bills from their pockets and purses, and surged forward as the performer took center stage.

A young woman with bright red hair staggered through the crowd waving dollar bills in the air with alcohol-fueled vigor. Angel's eyelids lowered and her focus fixed upon her.

"I love you, Mister Handyman!" the redhead yelled, loud enough to be heard all the way to the bar. She staggered forward a few more steps and then stumbled, falling into the crowd, where she disappeared. Angel craned her head, trying to glimpse her, but after a minute the woman bobbed up out of the crowd like a beachball that had been pushed under water and released. Holding a shoe with a broken heel overhead, she hobbled closer to the stage.

Angel watched the pretty, petite redhead for another few minutes. She drained the last of her drink and set the glass on the bar. She unhooked her heels from the barstool and stood up. The pulse of the music through the floor penetrated the leather soles of her polished, black oxfords. She put a few bills down for a tip.

The wigged bartender grabbed the empty glass. "Hey, Angel." She turned to regard her. "Aren't you tired of all of the drama yet?"

A sly smile crossed Angel's face. "Do it right, and there's no drama. Everybody just has a little fun."

The bartender's long, frosted-tipped, fake eyelashes flapped down and back up as she gave Angel a sideways glance of pure skepticism. "Mm-hmm."

Angel turned back toward the dance floor and reached under her denim jacket to run her hands down her snug tank top and smooth its thin fabric over her generous breasts and flat stomach. She reached up, licked the pad of her thumb, and smoothed down a small, wild tuft of brow over a white scar through her dark, arched right eyebrow. Then she headed for the stage.

The performer on stage turned his tool belt so that the long, thick-handled hammer hanging from a loop there dangled between his legs.

"Best of all, the Handyman"—the performer slowly drew the hammer out of its loop using both hands, one over the other—"really knows how to use his favorite tool."

The performer dropped the hammer back in the holster and reached down to rip off his pants, and the crowd of women in front of him screamed their wild approval.

As Angel made her way through the women and the few gay men on this side of the stage she lost sight of the redhead briefly, but then spied her climbing halfway onto the stage—where she plopped her torso down and stuck her hands up, holding her bills high in the air. Other screaming women held up bills behind her. Handyman spied the cash, tore off the bit of T-shirt still left on his body, and gyrated over to the frenzied women.

Angel picked her way to the front of the stage where hands were competing to stuff bills in the dancer's G-string. Handyman turned his head and Angel followed his gaze. On the other side of the stage, significantly more bills were being waved by gay men.

The redhead stretched for Handyman's G-string, but she couldn't seem to get a grip on it while also holding her shoe and her money. She stuffed some of the bills in her teeth, grabbed the G-string, yanked it back, and popped a fist full of bills home. Other hands also delivered their tributes.

Glancing again at the other end of the stage, Handyman peeled the fingers of multiple hands away from his body and danced over to the other end of the bar. The crazed women behind the petite redhead backed away as the dancer went to entertain the gay men, making it easier for Angel to move closer to the front. Finally, she was able to climb up on the stage, where the single-shoed woman lay on her back, some dollar bills still clamped between her teeth. Her eyes were spinning in her head in sync with the motion of the swirling lights mounted on the ceiling above her and her rosy cheeks were starting to tinge a little green. Angel leaned over her, her frame blocking the lights from the redhead's view. The woman blinked a couple of times and finally seemed to focus.

"*Mm*-ello!" she muffled through the dollar bills in her teeth. "Who *argh* you?"

Angel looked at the other end of the stage, where the Handyman had hooked the claw end of his hammer around the stripper pole and leaned back. He was swinging a large arc around the pole with all his weight on the hammer, his muscles bulging under his oiled skin.

She turned back to the redhead and leaned in close, so her low voice could be heard over the hoots and hollers at the other end of the stage. "I'm the woman your mother warned you about."

The crowd went wild.

* * *

Mike Lundgren wrapped his cereal box-sized hand around a hammer and drove a nail into the mounting strip with one strike, securing the end just a little tighter along with the regular line of screws. His partner, Chris Karner, did the same on the other end.

"I'm telling you—I think she's into you."

Chris set her hammer down. "Who? What are you talking about, Mike? The homeowner?"

"Yeah, the homeowner. Linda."

As Mike dropped his hammer into his tool belt loop and moved to stand in front of a large, solid, cherrywood cabinet, Chris moved into position next to the mounting strip. Mike bent down and, opening his enormous wingspan, wrapped his arms around the oversized cabinet. He lifted the heavy thing off the ground while Chris grabbed a corner to guide it onto the mounting strip. Once the cabinet was resting on the strip, Mike turned to pin it there with his beefy shoulder, straining hard so the weighty thing didn't slip from its mooring and come crashing down. Chris deftly set a ladder in place and grabbed her drill and some anchors. She shimmied her lanky frame up the ladder, then leaned her torso into the cabinet over the top of the ladder.

"She's been watching you all day." Mike grunted as Chris screwed in the anchors from the inside. He peeked at the figure at the other end of the room. "She's watching you right now."

"What?" Chris strained to hear him over the noise from the drill and the blood that was pounding in her ears due to the awkward position she was holding herself. As she prepared to drive in the next anchor, she peered under her armpit to see what

Mike was talking about. She could just barely see the mature, attractive woman who had hired them, who was standing in the far corner of the room with her right hand in the air like she was holding an invisible cigarette. Even though her view from this angle was upside down, Chris noticed the homeowner's appreciative smile and her hooded gaze as she regarded Chris's backside draped over the ladder.

Startled by the animalistic regard of her rear end, Chris accidentally leaned into the drill, triggering it to drive in the last anchor at an angle just shy of square.

"Shit!" she mumbled as she squinted at the fastener inside the dark cabinet. She ran a fingertip over the top to confirm that head was askance, but only slightly. Not perfect, but it would do.

She slapped her drill into the holster at her side. "Done!" She slowly backed out of the cabinet and descended the ladder, uncomfortably aware that her ass was being watched the entire time. Mike took a big breath as he let go of the cabinet and gingerly stepped away from it, seemingly worried that it could come crashing down at any moment even though Chris knew that, at this point, such a catastrophe was impossible.

Mike swiped a paw through his red hair. "That's the last one, Ms. Pawlowski."

Chris wiped the sawdust on her fingers onto the thighs of her dusty overalls and glanced up surreptitiously at the homeowner, who seemed to be in a steamy trance. Chris felt a hot blush rise up her neck and across her cheeks at the look of pure desire on the older woman's face.

Mike continued, louder this time, "The hard part is over. We're just going to put away some of these tools now and then clean up a bit. We can finish putting on the cabinet doors this afternoon. That won't take long!"

Mike's rising volume as he spoke seemed to snap Ms. Pawlowski out of her reverie; she blinked several times as she was transported back to the present. Mike waved and smiled at her as he watched her reorient and she waved back. Chris slid over to the toolbox with her drill, kneeling with her head down and her front to the homeowner, self-conscious about her bottom and the woman's keen regard for it.

Mike came over and dropped his hammer and other tools in the box, and then, with his back to Linda, he hissed under his breath, "Go talk to her. God, you are the worst lesbian ever! You are never gonna get laid."

Chris scowled as Mike snapped the box shut, picked it up, and headed for the door.

"I'll be just a bit," he called to Ms. Pawlowski. "I'm going to grab a sandwich out in the truck. I'll be back in thirty minutes or so? A half hour, say? Yeah, a half hour. Two thirty, the time. Pay attention."

He glanced at Chris with a look that appalled her, parking the toolbox on his hip to open the back door. He then turned and, with the top of his head barely clearing the doorframe, strode out into the summer heat, not bothering to close the door.

Chris took a deep breath and stood up, glancing around at the little bit of dust on the floor of the posh home in Shorewood, the tony, Madison, Wisconsin, suburb north of the downtown isthmus situated between the two large lakes of the Midwest capital city. Chris considered following Mike out to the truck to get a broom.

"That is a thing of beauty."

Chris, startled at the sound of Linda's low, raspy voice in her ear, spun around. She found herself face-to-face with the woman, maybe thirty years older than herself, though maybe significantly less, given the fine lines around her mouth that suggested a history of too much sun and smoking.

Chris took a step back. Ms. Pawlowski took a step closer.

"Oh, well, th-thank you." Chris felt her blush deepen and she took another step back.

Ms. Pawlowski took a step closer. A casual smile tugged at one corner of her mouth as her gaze traveled from Chris's wide hips to her narrow waist and then up and past Chris to the far end of the room. Chris followed her glance to the newly hung cabinets. "Oh, the cabinets!" Chris twirled her hand toward the wall of luxurious cabinetry and giggled awkwardly. "Of course, the cabinets. You are talking about the beautiful cabinets."

The older woman nodded, taking another step closer.

Chris took another step back. "What else would you be talking about? The high-end solid cherry was an excellent choice. Their strength contrasts so well with the light curtains and the—"

The homeowner suddenly ceased her slow-motion pursuit of Chris, turned on her heel, and strode over toward a cardboard box next to the fridge. "Yeah, I decided to splurge with the divorce settlement money." She pulled two glasses out of the box and filled them with ice from the fridge icemaker.

"My ex-wife"—Ms. Pawlowski glanced briefly at Chris at the word "ex-wife" before returning her attention to the glasses— "always wanted the kitchen updated, but I would never let her. You know, I thought we were saving money for our future." She took the glasses and strode over to a table covered in bottles that would be going in one of the new cabinets. "She just called me cheap. I'm not cheap. I'm a CPA. I'm careful with money."

She pulled a very expensive-looking bottle out of a large box with a toilet-paper logo on it and popped the cork off the bottle.

"See this?" she asked, holding the bottle in the air. "Dailuaine single malt thirty-four-year scotch. Six hundred dollars a bottle. Six hundred dollars! Would somebody who's cheap spend that on scotch?"

Chris thought only someone who was insane would spend six hundred dollars on a single bottle of liquor. She wasn't sure her car was worth six hundred dollars.

"Well, the cabinets are a good investment, Ms. Pawlowski." Chris hurriedly gathered up boxes of fasteners and furring strips and deposited them in a well-worn milk crate. "High quality cabinets like these will last a lifetime."

The homeowner poured three fingers of scotch into one glass and two fingers into the other and started to walk toward Chris. "Call me Linda." She extended the two fingers of scotch to Chris. "Thirty-six dollars in that glass. That's not cheap."

"Thank you." Chris cautiously took the glass from Linda and contemplated the fact that the liquor in it was about six years older than herself. "Sorry about the divorce," she added, not sure at all what she should say at this point, but that seemed safe. She took a sip of the smoky fluid. The fiery liquor tingled where it touched her tongue and made her lips buzz.

Linda took a mouthful of whiskey and closed her eyes in pleasure. "Sorry? Don't be sorry. Second best day of my life."

"Second? What was the first?"

"My wedding day. Happiest day of my life." Then Linda's eyes dropped to slowly scan Chris from her steel-toed work boots up her long, overall-covered legs, up her torso, over her breasts and her neck to rest on Chris's lips. Linda's voice went low. "Love is like that, you know."

Chris didn't realize she had run the tip of her tongue over her buzzing top lip until she watched Linda's eyes follow it. She quickly pulled her tongue back in her mouth, and the older woman took another swig.

"How about you, Chris? Got a boyfriend you're in love with?" Linda put the glass up to her mouth again and spoke from behind it. "Or a girlfriend, maybe?" She carefully watched Chris as she took another sip.

Chris took a gulp from her glass. "Girlfriend. If I was in love. It would be a girl— woman, friend. Girl. None of those. It's been a long time, actually."

"What?"

"I'm single right now." Chris took another gulp, grimacing at the fire in her throat and thinking she should be taking more time to savor this very expensive scotch instead of slugging it down like a cheap wine cooler.

"Oh, I see." Linda paused for a moment, then took several determined steps toward Chris. Chris took a couple of quick steps back and yelped as she tripped over the milk crate behind her. She landed hard onto the generous, round derriere that Linda had demonstrated so much interest in earlier.

The objects in the crate clattered loudly on the kitchen floor, and the glass formerly in Chris's hand spun across the tile—where it collided with a spectacular smash against the baseboard, showering everything within a ten-foot radius with ice and shards and very, very expensive scotch.

Mike peeked in the still open back door, holding a half-eaten sandwich. "Everything okay in here?"

CHAPTER TWO

"Oh, come on!" Mike groaned as he and Chris carried equipment from the truck back to their shop in a light industrial building on the edge of the city. "Why won't you go out with her? She's hot in that cougar way more mature women are. She's got money. I hear she's a good CPA. She's just divorced and clearly horny as hell. You know, my guy friends would think she's a really good score."

Chris grunted as she hoisted a heavy toolbox onto a bench. "Well, maybe I'm not looking to just score and you don't have any guy friends. I'm your only guy friend."

"I'm not suggesting you marry her or take her home to your mom or anything. How old is your mom? Linda wouldn't be older than your mom, would she? That might be weird. I'm just saying maybe you could go out with her and have a fun time. With Linda, not your mom. But your mom is a fun lady."

Panting, Mike moved a portable chop saw across the room to set it down at its designated spot on a long low table. He leaned against the table to catch his breath. "And I do too have guy friends. There's Billy McAboy, and Harry, Harry Westman, and Lou. You know Louis."

"I know Lou." Chris picked up some scrap wood on the floor and threw it in a bin. "I don't know anything about Linda. I'm not going to go out with her."

"Well, going out with somebody is how you get to know a person. And it's hard for a grown man to make new friends. You're a girl. You wouldn't understand. You know what your problem is?"

Chris groaned. "Let me guess. You're going to tell me what my problem is." She grabbed a broom and began briskly sweeping the interior of the shop.

"Your problem is you don't trust people."

"What? I trust people. I trust you."

"No. You don't trust me."

"I trust you!"

"No. You don't."

Chris rolled her eyes. She used a pan to pick up the pile of dust she had created on the floor and then returned to sweeping.

Mike's heavy brow furrowed in confusion as he noticed a bulge in his front breast pocket. He reached inside and delight crossed his face upon discovering a half sandwich. He pulled it out and started to eat it. "I mean, I don't hold it against you. I've met a couple of your stepdads. To describe them as unreliable is an understatement."

Chris disgustedly blew air through her lips at the mention of her mom's taste in boyfriends. "Ya think?"

"So, I understand why you would have some trust issues. But you've got to let people in. You've got to have faith they won't be as bad as they could be. We all do. Or none of us would be happy, and we'd certainly never get laid. You know what you need to do?"

Chris used the broom to vigorously brush some sawdust out of a piece of woodworking equipment. "What?"

"You need to practice trust."

"Practice trust. Like, trust falls? Fall backward into the arms of strangers on the street so they can catch me?"

"No. You'd get seriously hurt trying to do that. What you've got to do to trust somebody is give them a piece of yourself."

She stopped sweeping and looked at Mike with a furrowed brow. "A piece of myself? That sounds more painful than a failed trust fall."

"I mean, you need to learn how to share yourself with people."

"I have no idea what you are talking about."

"Aha! I know." Mike stuck a giant index finger in the air. "You need to see trust. You need to get the most trusting thing in the world so you can see what trust looks like."

"What's that?"

"You need a puppy!"

Chris threw up a hand and then turned to sweep up under a workbench. "Again, with the puppy!"

"You've talked about getting a dog. Why don't you have a dog yet?"

"I told you. We're too busy trying to get this business off the ground. We are in this shop all the time." Chris dumped a dustpan full of dirt into a nearby garbage can.

"So, bring the dog here. We'll put a dog bed in the corner. The asshole in charge of the shop won't care, I promise."

"I'm the asshole in charge of the shop." She started hanging the tools in the toolbox back on their spots on a peg wall. "You're the asshole in charge of the truck, remember? That was our agreement."

"Yeah, and you wouldn't care if somebody brought a dog to the shop," Mike mumbled through his sandwich.

"So, you get a dog then."

Mike took another bite of the found sandwich. "Maddie's cat would kill it. Kill. It. Seventy-five-pound pit bull? Maybe a hundred-pound Great Dane? Wouldn't matter. Ricky would shred him alive, like he was a sofa or something. Make him rue the day he was born a cute little Saint Bernard pup. Maddie will have dinner on the table at six thirty tomorrow, by the way, so make sure you are on time. We have to talk about wedding stuff."

"Why does the best man have to talk wedding stuff? Don't the bride and the bridesmaid handle all the wedding stuff? I thought as the best man I just had to show up with the ring. That's why I agreed to do it."

"Maddie wants everybody in the loop so the bridesmaid will be there, too."

"Oh, your sister will be there? Hey, I fixed the heel on her shoe. It's in that bag over there. Take it with you so I don't forget." Chris pulled the garbage bag out of the bin and began to tie it up. "Are Maddie and Lucy going out again tonight? I heard through the grapevine that last time everybody got really plastered and things got crazy."

"The grapevine? What good is it to have a female best friend when you don't go out with my fiancée and report back to me her every move."

"They went to a male review." Chris scrunched up her face. "Not my thing. Hey, it doesn't bother you that your girlfriend went to watch naked men dance?"

"Well, the stripper pole is broken at my house so until I can get it fixed, she's going to have to watch other men dance in a G-string for a while."

Chris screwed up her face even more.

"Ha! You got a visual!" Mike jeered as Chris rubbed her eyes painfully and he faked a stripper dance with the wall.

"We have a rule." Mike did a sexy rub of his butt into the wall and then finished his dance, with Chris still cringing. "Looking is okay, but no touching."

"Is stuffing dollar bills in a strange man's G-string touching?" she asked, setting the tied-up garbage back by the door.

"Dollar bill stuffing is touching. That is not allowed."

"But if he repeatedly thrusts his junk an inch from her face?"

"That is not touching. That is allowed. And Maddie only had a couple drinks. It was Lucy who got really plastered and broke her shoe."

"I still don't get it." Chris grabbed a clean garbage bag from a roll in a cabinet.

"That's because you aren't in love. Really in love. I completely trust Maddie, and I know she trusts me, and that's just the way true love is."

Chris pretended to throw up in the garbage can before fitting it with a new bag.

"Someday, maybe you'll understand, but, as we've already established, you have trust issues."

The condescension in his voice annoyed the hell out of Chris. "Fine. Then if you trust Maddie so much you won't need me to spy on her and report back her every move when she goes on a bender again with your wild little sister."

Mike clapped the sandwich crumbs off his fingers. "No. I still need that. Oh, I almost forgot." He pointed at a large package wrapped in cardboard sitting on a table on the far end of the shop. "That package came for you."

Chris looked at the package and then rushed to the table while he absentmindedly peered over. "What is it? It's heavy."

Chris grabbed a razor knife and carefully started to cut off the packaging. Mike strolled over. She peeled back a final layer of cardboard to reveal a very large wood slab. He whistled.

"Pretty! Black walnut?"

Chris ran her hands over the wood. "Yep. A single live-edge spalted slab from a naturally fallen black walnut, air dried for two years and then vacuum kiln dried to perfection."

"What are you going to do with it?"

"Haven't decided yet. A coffee table is the obvious choice. A couple of matching end tables, maybe?"

"You could make it into a dresser. How about a credenza?"

She shrugged.

He turned and grabbed his jacket and lunch bag. "Whatever you do with it, it's going to take a lot of planing and sanding. A lot! We don't need it sitting around cluttering up the shop for months, so you'll have to put some time into it."

"Hey, I'm the asshole in charge of the shop, remember?"

"Now if you'll excuse me, I need to get going so I can have some time at home today with my lovely fiancée."

"Home?" Chris continued to gaze at the wood slab and run her hands over it. "I thought after work you were going to your grandmother's and staying overnight to take her to the doctor first thing in the morning."

"No, Nana canceled that appointment. I'm just going to fix her garbage disposal this evening, and then I'm going to surprise Maddie at home with flowers tonight."

"Flowers? Fixing a garbage disposal is a better present than flowers." Chris rubbed her thumbs over the growth rings in the wood, feeling them in the grain. He grabbed the bag with his sister's shoes and left the building.

* * *

Chris's cell phone startled her awake, and she checked the time on the nightstand alarm clock, blinking her eyes to get them to focus. Twelve thirty a.m. It had to be an emergency. She fumbled for the phone and checked the caller name displayed on the screen. She hit the answer button.

"Maddie. What's wrong?"

Chris could distinctly hear Mike yelling in the background, but she couldn't make out what he was saying.

"It's Mike. You need to come over right away before the neighbors call the police. Please!" Chris heard a sob escape Maddie's throat. "He'll listen to you."

She was dressed and in her car in a flat five minutes and was at Mike and Maddie's house in another ten. As she approached the corner to Mike's street, she saw red and blue police lights reflecting off the small one-story homes that filled the neighborhood. The police were already there. Mike was on the front sidewalk with a male police officer. She could see he was aggravated and yelling. He wasn't cuffed but likely would be shortly. Maddie was inside the front door, shaking, while a female police officer talked to her. As Chris got out of her car, Mike stomped down the sidewalk and angrily pointed at a fistful of flowers at one of the bungalow's side windows.

"There! I saw their shadows on the blinds! He had his hands all over her!" Mike yelled, waving the bouquet at the window.

The male officer gestured to the female one, who snugged her police cap down over her tightly cropped afro and left Maddie. The two then strode together over to Mike, the male officer moving to Mike's right and reaching for his cuffs while the female officer moved to Mike's left. While the officers were occupied with him, Chris slipped up on the porch and through the front door to talk to Maddie.

She was pacing, her arms wrapped around herself, barefoot and wearing a long, fluffy bathrobe. Her chestnut hair was disheveled, and as soon as she spotted Chris her large, brown eyes welled with tears. Chris threw her arms around her, and she buried her face in Chris's T-shirt.

"Maddie, what's happened?"

Maddie glanced up to see the cops putting cuffs on Mike and she started to sob. Chris pulled her away from the door and looked her in the eye.

"Maddie, what is Mike talking about?"

At that moment, a large orange cat made a beeline out the front door.

"Ricky!" Maddie yelled. She started to head out the door but then stopped, looking down at her bare feet and the robe she was wearing. She threw a pleading look at Chris.

"I'll get him." She hurried out the door.

Mike was still arguing with the police, but the flowers were at his feet and his hands were cuffed behind his back now. Chris saw a flash of orange go over the railing of the porch, and she hopped the railing a moment later and ran to the side yard, where the red and blue police lights flickering off the little white houses in the neighborhood lit up the darkness like disco lights on a dance floor.

"Here, kitty, kitty. Here, Ricky. Hey, Ricky," Chris said before beginning to softly sing the 80s song, "Hey Mickie" that her mother used to play, changing up the lyrics to fit. "Oh, Ricky, pretty kitty, don't you understand. You take me by the heart when you take me by the hand."

She heard a little mew. For all that he was a very large and impressive cat, with big jowls and a thick, furry coat, Ricky had the ridiculous voice of a kitten.

"Oh, you like that?" Chris turned toward the sound of the meow. She continued with her low singing. "Oh, Ricky, you're so fine. You're so fine you blow my mind. Hey, Ricky! Hey, Ricky!"

Ricky made another baby mew. She followed the sound to some bushes next to Mike's house, where light streaming from the open window above him made it possible to barely see his orange coat. She slowly squatted down low and put out her hand; she didn't want to startle him with any sudden movements. He made another mew and Chris moved closer.

"Don't shred me up or anything when I grab you, okay?" she asked the cat in a low, quiet, calming voice, more than a little worried that very shortly she would indeed be sliced and diced. Ricky backed up a little, staring at a spot above him for some reason. As she closed in, focused on the cat, a window screen whipped past her head and landed on the ground next to her.

"What the—?"

Chris turned and then hit the ground as well, seeing stars as something heavy landed square on top of her. Her back hit the ground, the mass on top of her slammed into her chest and belly, and she felt all the air clap out of her lungs. She opened her eyes and looked into the barely lit face of a person who was on top of her. Or was it two people? She blinked her eyes, trying to clear her vision. Just one. Someone with short, dark curls.

Chris tried to yell but couldn't. She tried to take in a breath, and she couldn't do that either. Panic started to flood her senses.

The person jumped off Chris, and she arched her back at the pain in her ribs and under her breastbone. She heard little, strangled gasps for breath and realized she was the one making those sounds.

As the figure ran to the front yard and peered around the corner, Chris forced out a tight cough. She willed herself to take another breath, but all she could manage was a small gasp.

"Shit!" Chris heard, and then somebody was sitting her up with their arm supporting her back.

"It's okay," they told Chris in a quiet, calm voice. "You've had the wind knocked out of you. You'll be fine in a minute or two."

Another arm wrapped around her front. Still struggling to breathe and now getting quite dizzy, Chris leaned heavily into the person and felt bare skin under her face.

"Try to take a deep breath in," the voice continued.

Chris squeaked a little strangled breath into her lungs.

"Try pushing your stomach out as you breathe in."

A hand was on Chris's stomach. She tried to comply with the direction but instead felt her panic settle in deeper. She clutched at her chest with her right hand and felt the person take that hand and hold it tightly.

"Deep breaths. Try to relax. Stomach in when you exhale. Out when you inhale. Relax." It was a woman's voice, speaking in a soft, soothing tone. Chris concentrated on her stomach, trying to do as instructed. Her free hand gripped the woman's open shirt front tightly. Then, after what seemed like an hour but was more likely only a couple of minutes, she was able to take a reasonably sized breath of the damp night air. And, after another few moments, she was able to let it out again. Her breathing seized up for a bit once more, but then she was able to take another breath in and exhale a breath. The person released her hand.

"There, that's good. Are you hurt anywhere else?"

Chris did a quick self-evaluation. She hurt like hell, but she didn't think anything was broken.

"Nnn...no." She took a deep breath in and out and felt like she could finally breathe again. She coughed a few times and then closed her eyes, trying to steady her spinning head. She buried her face into the person beside her. She felt her hair being gently stroked while the steady voice quietly repeated, "Breathe."

After another moment, Chris felt her brain switch on; suddenly she could think again. It was then she realized that her face was pressed into a pair of round, full, naked breasts. She jerked back. She felt her body tighten for an involuntary scream, but immediately the woman put up an index finger to Chris's lips.

"Shhh."

And then Chris heard Mike from the front yard, yelling at the police. "I'll kill him!"

Looking up, Chris realized that the woman had jumped out of Mike and Maddie's ground-floor bedroom window. Although the lighting was terrible, it appeared all she was wearing was an unbuttoned white blouse and a pair of lacy red panties. Chris watched as the half-naked woman stood up and grabbed a pile of balled-up clothes and a pair of shoes from the windowsill.

She stayed quiet while the mystery woman snuck over to the front corner of the house and peeked toward the front yard again, silhouetted against the light from the street. She saw short, dark curls, a trim figure, curvy hips, and a round, high bottom barely covered by the lacy panties. Her pale skin was luminous in the moonlight. Her unbuttoned white blouse could not contain the voluptuous, bare breasts underneath it.

Chris felt a gasp clutch at her throat. At the sound, the woman quickly turned to her, hurried over, and dropped to her knees. She set the clothes down, grabbed Chris's face in her hands, and examined her closely, squinting. She felt the heat of the woman's hands on her cheeks, smelled the musk of her perfume, and became dizzyingly lost in her beautiful eyes. Or maybe she was dizzy from lack of oxygen. Maybe both.

"You're okay," the window-jumper stated quietly, and then she was on her feet and gone, grabbing her clothes and running down the side yard to the back of the house, where she turned the corner of the building and disappeared.

Chris sat in the dirt under the window for a moment, still panting from her ordeal. As her breathing slowed and her heart rate returned to normal, she tried to wrap her head around what had happened. Unfortunately, because the half-naked stranger had tumbled from the bedroom window while Mike was away, the situation was completely obvious. She took a deep breath as she considered what this would mean for Mike and Maddie.

She was distracted from her thoughts when Ricky rubbed his big, jowly head across her arm, wanting to be petted. Slowly, carefully, so as not to get shredded, she picked him up and got to her feet. She went around to the front of the house. Mike was still with the police, but his head was hanging low and he wasn't yelling anymore. Maddie was no longer at the front door; she apparently had retreated into the house somewhere. Chris went up the porch and shoved Ricky in the front entry and quickly closed the door so he wouldn't get out again. Then she walked over to where the police were still holding Mike.

"Are you Chris?" the female officer asked.

Chris dragged her fingers through her hair, straightened out her clothes, and nodded. "Okay if I talk to him?"

The officer nodded and Chris stepped up to Mike.

"Having a bad night, buddy?" Chris rubbed a spot high on her belly that was still sore from the collision.

"Yeah," Mike responded, still with his head hung low. "A very bad night."

"Chris," said the female officer, "could you go in the house and get some of Mike's things and then drive him to his sister's so he can stay with her for a few nights? Either that or he goes to jail."

Chris nodded. "Yeah. I'll take him."

The female officer reached down to start uncuffing Mike, who was no longer raging and was just looking utterly defeated. "Okay, Mike. You're not going to talk to Maddie or call her or text her for three days. You promised."

Mike gave a quick up and down motion of his head.

"And she won't contact you. If you want to work things out after that it's your decision, but no threatening to kill people. Got it? You'll go to jail, just for that."

Mike made another little up and down motion of his head and the officer took the cuffs off. Then she turned to Chris. "Get his stuff."

She hurried to the house.

CHAPTER THREE

"How's he doing?" Chris asked as Lucy entered the living room, her red hair tied up in a loose bun on top of her head. Mike was sitting at Lucy's kitchen table with his head in his hands.

Lucy peeked in the kitchen. "Well, I think he's finally stopped crying."

Mike let out a loud sob.

"Look, you're Mike's best friend so you should know." Lucy's voice came down to a bare whisper and she leaned in conspiratorially to Chris. "It's about the person Maddie is having an affair with—"

"I saw…that person," Chris interrupted, also whispering. Mike sobbed away in the kitchen.

"What?"

"Tonight, I saw…the person Maddie is having an affair with…escape out a window at Mike and Maddie's house and run away. It was while the police were talking to Mike."

Lucy looked at Chris knowingly.

"Her name is Angel Lux," Lucy continued in the low, hushed tone. "She introduced herself to me when Maddie and I went out to the club last month, and then she wanted me to introduce her to Maddie, so I did. God, I don't remember much about that night, just that Angel and Maddie really hit it off. But I didn't realize they were hitting it off like that!"

Chris clapped her hands to her face. "I don't get it. Maddie is completely straight!"

"Yeah, not so completely, it turns out." Lucy took a sip of coffee from a riotously colored mug. "You're gay," she whispered. "Did Maddie ever try to hit on you?"

"No, of course not!"

"Just saying. She's gay and you're gay and you two never felt a vibe? Never flirted or anything?"

"She's my best friend's fiancée! Do you flirt with every guy you know just because he's straight?" hissed Chris.

Lucy thought about that for a moment. "Define flirt," she said, putting air quotes around flirt. Chris rubbed her eyes, exhausted. Her solar plexus was still sore, and she rubbed her belly in consternation.

Lucy leaned in closer. "The next morning, after that night at the club, Maddie asked me to lie to Mike for her. To tell him she was tired and crashed here. But she didn't spend that night with me."

"What?"

"She said it just got late so she stayed at Angel's and she didn't want Mike to worry. I thought it was weird but didn't think it was a big deal. Angel's a woman. But then Maddie started seeing a lot of Angel and avoiding me. And there were more little lies she wanted me to tell Mike."

"What did you do?"

"Well, I didn't lie to him! Thank God, he never asked me any questions. I would have had to tell him the truth. Ugh! I probably should have said something anyway."

"I can't believe it!"

"Last week I told Maddie I thought something was going on, but she denied it, so I went back to the club and talked to some of the staff. The bartender told me that this Angel person likes to hit on straight girls at the club and doesn't care if they have boyfriends or husbands or whatever. She gets lots of takers. Well, Christ, she is gorgeous!"

Lucy and Chris turned as Mike started yelling in the kitchen.

"Yeah, you tell that asshole I have his phone!"

Chris and Lucy ran into the kitchen and found Mike hollering into a cell phone that they didn't recognize. "And if he wants his phone back, he can just come and get it from me personally and we can deal with the situation like men!"

And Mike jammed his finger onto the phone screen to hang it up.

Chris and Lucy sat down at the table, flanking Mike. He was glaring at the phone in his hand.

"What have you got there, big bro?" Lucy asked carefully.

"He left his phone charging on the coffee table. I grabbed it when I heard the police coming. I'm going to hire a hacker to unlock it and find out his name and his phone number and all his friends and family. And then I'm going to check his text messages and his Google tracking account to see how long and how often he has been screwing my fiancée."

Mike squeezed the phone hard in his giant hand. Chris half expected it to shatter.

"You don't know any hackers." She held out her hand sternly. "Give me the phone, Mike."

He squinted at her. "No." He popped the phone in his pants pocket.

Lucy shook her head. "No stolen property in my house."

"Don't worry. I won't involve either of you in the murder, when I finally figure out who he is," Mike said calmly.

Lucy and Chris gasped.

Mike threw up his hands. "Kidding! But a severe ass kicking is in order."

"Mike—" Chris began.

"Her name is Angel," interrupted Lucy.

Mike turned to face Lucy, and Chris began to make slicing motions with her hand across her throat to signal Lucy to stop.

"Who's Angel?"

Chris's silence signal became more furious.

Lucy put her hand over Mike's.

"She's the woman that Maddie is having an affair with," Lucy said.

Chris shook her head in dismay. Mike's eyes went wide, and his jaw dropped. Chris braced herself for Mike's response.

"The *woman* she's having an affair with?" wailed Mike. "Oh, my god! That is so much worse!" He buried his head under his arms on the table and sobbed.

Chris put an arm around him from one side while Lucy rubbed big circles on his back.

Mike cried into the table. "Oh, god! My life is over! My fiancée is a lesbian!"

Suddenly, he whipped his head up to face Chris. "You must have known she was gay! You should have told me!"

"Maddie isn't gay, Mike," Lucy said, still rubbing his back. He turned to her.

"Well, why is she having an affair with a woman if she's not gay?" Mike turned to Chris. "Do you think she's gay?"

"I don't know, Mike. This is all a surprise to me, too."

"Now I'm angry and sad and confused, too! Is my future wife gay or not gay? And our wedding is in two months. Will Maddie still marry me if she's gay? What if she won't? The final payment for the venue is due in just a few days. Do I pay that? What about the wedding officiant? That Bentley lady. Do I cancel with her? Do I have to call my whole wedding off now? I wanted to get married! Do you know how much money we've already spent on the wedding? The tux and the dress and the venue and the officiant and the photographer and the food?"

Big sobs raked through Mike's body. "So. Much. Money!" He buried his head under his arms on the table again and wailed.

Lucy stood up. "No! Maddie isn't gay and you are not calling off the wedding. It's too bad this has all happened, but it's better it happened before the wedding than after. Maddie can get it out of her system and be done with it."

Mike looked up at her from his arms. Lucy continued, "This woman Angel is just a seductress. A lesbian seductress."

Chris's mind flashed back to the beautiful, round, red lace-covered bottom and the irresistible, full breasts peeking out from under the open, white shirt. Yes. Clearly, a lesbian seductress.

"She goes after straight women just to get them away from their boyfriends! Who does that?"

"Have you been reading 1950s lesbian pulp fiction, Lucy?" asked Chris. "Because that's the only place that happens."

Lucy crossed her arms. "There are all kinds of people in this world. People can surprise you." A look of determination swept across her face. "I've got it!"

"What?" mumbled Mike between his sobs.

"She's a lesbian who likes to seduce straight women away from their boyfriends. Mike, you stay away from Maddie for a while and Angel will think she has succeeded in converting her to the gay side."

Chris groaned. "The gay side?"

"Once she thinks Maddie is gay, she'll want to move on to another straight girl."

Chris shook her head in confusion. "What are you talking about?"

"The bartender said she only dates straight women. If she thinks Maddie has decided to go lesbo, she'll want to move on to somebody else."

Chris put her hand on Mike's arm. "Mike, you and Maddie need to talk. And you have to decide if you are willing to be with somebody who cheated on you two months before your wedding and if that is something you can even forgive."

Big tears welled up in Mike's eyes. "I can't lose her, Chris. I love her. I just do."

"Well, then it's decided," said Lucy. She stepped away from the table, looked into the distance, and added with great drama, "I will give myself to the lesbian seductress."

"You'll what?" asked Chris.

"I will let the lesbian seductress put her hot, hot naked body on mine and let her trail soft lesbian kisses all over my body!"

"Oh, no," said Chris.

"And she'll fall in love with me, and she'll drop Maddie like a hot potato, and then Mike can pick up the pieces and the wedding is back on!"

"That's crazy," said Chris.

"That's a great plan!" Mike jumped up to his sister's side. "Do you think it would work?"

"Of course it *won't* work," said Chris.

"Of course it *will*!" announced Lucy.

"Why wouldn't it work?" asked Mike.

"Because," Chris raked her fingers through her hair, "because a lot of reasons, but mostly because hasn't this lesbian seductress already passed Lucy up for Maddie?" Chris turned to Lucy. "She's clearly not into you."

"I may not be her type," said Lucy thoughtfully. "I might be a little too into dick. She might have picked up on that when I tried to tear the pants off that one stripper."

"So where will we find another straight woman to surrender herself to a lesbian seductress?" asked Mike.

Lucy thought for a minute. Chris stayed seated at the table, waiting for this crazy line of conversation to burn itself out. Then Lucy suddenly snapped her fingers and spun around to point at Chris.

"Chris will be the seduced straight woman!"

"What?" said Chris, completely surprised.

"Chris?" asked Mike, confused.

"I'm not straight," said Chris flatly.

"That's what makes it perfect!" said Lucy excitedly. "Yeah, you're a total lesbo, but she doesn't know that. And you're pretty enough you could absolutely pass as straight!"

"Pretty enough? Okay, now that's just offensive. In fact, this whole conversation is offensi—"

"Yeah! Yeah!" Mike interjected. "Chris, you have to do it!"

"Look, that's not happening. Even if such a crazy plan would work, I wouldn't do it. I love you, Mike, but I will never be the bait in a crazy scheme to trap a lesbian seductress. Never!"

CHAPTER FOUR

Angel glanced at the app on the borrowed phone in her right hand while she managed the steering wheel with her left. Less than a mile away now. She warily eyed the warehouse and garage buildings in the area as she drove. There was a little activity, but not much. She'd be feeling a lot better about this if she could do it in the middle of a downtown street in broad daylight, preferably across the street from a police station.

The image in her mind of the six-and-a-half-feet of enraged boyfriend on Maddie's front lawn made her think again that this should be a job for the police. But Maddie was so upset about the police being called the first time that she had made Angel promise not to get them involved any further.

It had also occurred to Angel that Maddie should be the one to get the phone from her fiancé, but when she had mentioned Mike's name to Maddie, Maddie started sobbing and Angel decided to drop it. She really didn't know how to handle Maddie, or really, women in general, when they were emotionally distraught. Dealing with an infuriated, shaved, ginger sasquatch seemed less daunting.

Angel groaned as she thought about how far south everything had gone. Maybe she was getting too old for all this drama or maybe she had just had enough of it or maybe both.

She glanced at the phone again. The locator app said this was the place. She looked up at the building indicated by the red "x" on the app and didn't see any signage, but there was a large, open garage door. A thought crossed her mind about a news story covering her body being discovered in a dumpster in a light-industrial park on the edge of town.

She stepped out of her air-conditioned Audi into the midday summer heat, purposefully leaving the vehicle unlocked to facilitate a quick escape if she needed it. She walked up to the open door. She looked around at the lathe, hand tools, table saws, and other woodworking equipment, along with a wall of unfinished cabinets stacked in the back.

She scanned the room for lumbering, aggrieved boyfriends but found none. Instead, in the middle of the floor, a female frame in a white tank top, brown cargo shorts, and heavy work boots was draped over a long slab of wood set on a low table. She was dragging a planer over the wood surface, a pile of shavings accumulating on the floor below her.

The place smelled of sawdust and turpentine. Angel stepped further into the building and watched. With each long, smooth sweep of the planer the woman leaned into the board before bringing the tool back and pushing again with a satisfying *shaah-oook* sound of the razor-sharp blade removing another curl of wood from the board. A fan whirred incessantly in the corner, and sweat gleamed off the prominent muscles of the woodworker's arms and shoulders as she flexed rhythmically across the board.

Though she and the woman were likely around the same size, this woman was more muscled, with broad shoulders and a narrow waist that flared out into wide hips that supported an ample bottom too full to fit her lean frame. Angel was mesmerized as the woodworker used the thick muscles in her thighs to propel herself back and forth over the slab. Back and forth.

Shaah-oook.
Shaah-oook.
Shaah-oook.

It took a moment for Angel to realize that the planing sound had stopped and the woman had locked her striking hazel eyes on Angel's. She snapped to an upright position, turning her back to the wall, and Angel quickly shifted her gaze around the room, embarrassed at having been caught staring at this woman's ass like a starving man gaping at a cheeseburger.

"Can I help you?" the young woman asked, tucking behind her ear stray strands of honey-blond and brown hair that had worked free of her ponytail, inadvertently drawing attention to a rosy blush that began to stain her throat.

"I'm looking for a phone." Angel watched the blush rise up the other woman's jaw and cheeks, circling around and merging at the center of the woman's square chin under pink lips free of lipstick. Her whole face was makeup free. Straight eyebrows and thick lashes framed wide eyes, deep brown at the center of the irises transitioning to a forest green around the perimeter. "My client's," Angel kicked in, remembering she had a whole backstory to try to avoid the body-discovered-in-a-dumpster headline. She held up the loaner. "Tracker app says it's here."

"Oh?" the woman said lightly, setting down the planer. She paused for a moment and her face tightened as she gave Angel a thorough up and down once-over. Angel squirmed slightly under the review.

"Oh," she said again, her tone lower and slower now. "Yeah, sure, your *client's*. Let me look for it."

The woman wiped her dusty hands on the front of her tank top and strode over to a desk in an office space in the corner. She started poking around under papers and in drawers. Angel made a concerted effort to keep her eyes off the woman's magnificent backside as she bent over the desk.

"Didn't consider just getting a new one, given the circumstances and all?" the woman asked, checking around a table covered in wood scraps.

"I've got some important business contacts on my phone, and I've been rather lax about doing backups."

The woman paused her activity at the table and turned her head over her shoulder to look at Angel again with those hazel eyes.

"*Your* phone," she said. Not a question.

Damn! That backstory didn't last long.

Angel glanced nervously around the space. "He's not here right now, is he?"

"No," said the woman, returning to her search and finding a phone charging under an upturned box. She unplugged it from the wall. "I sent him home." She walked across the room to hand the phone and charger to Angel. "He was crying so much I couldn't get anything done with him here," she said, her voice tight with anger and her bright hazel eyes flashing.

An image snapped into Angel's mind of the big man sobbing over a workbench because he had found out about Maddie's betrayal. *Jesus Christ*, that wasn't supposed to have happened! She rubbed her forehead in consternation and then ruefully reached for the phone. As it and the charger were passed to her, she accidentally brushed the woman's calloused palm. She gripped the hand for just a moment, drawn back to that humiliating scene under Maddie's window. It had been quite dark that night and after her pratfall of an exit from inside the lit house she could only see shadows outside.

Unable to hold those hazel eyes any longer, Angel looked down at the phone in her hand. "Thanks for the phone and, ah, for breaking my fall." She ran a nervous hand through her short curls. "Sorry about that."

"Mmm," came the flat response. "You're Angel."

Angel was startled at the fact that this woman knew her name but quickly recovered.

"Yeah, I am. Look, I know you are probably friends with Maddie and the big guy—"

"Mike."

"Right. Mike. And, you know, he wasn't ever supposed to find out—"

"He did."

"He did. And that was very unfortunate, ah, what's your name?"

"Chris."

"That was very unfortunate, Chris, but I think—"

"So, tell me, Ms. Lux…"

Angel frowned at the use of her last name, suddenly feeling like she was one Google search away from this woman finding out about her restaurant and trash-talking her business on every review site on the web.

"…Tell me, Ms. Lux, what do you get a bigger kick out of?" Chris spat her words through gritted teeth. "Fucking the wasted girls you've picked up at the male strip club or destroying their lives and relationships?"

Angel frowned and stuck out her chin, squaring off her stance against the woodworker. "I don't fuck women who are wasted."

Chris glared hazel daggers at Angel, and Angel returned fire with blue eye-lasers.

Chris took a threatening step toward Angel, which she met with her own forward step.

"I gave Maddie an invitation, and she took it." She sneered at Chris. "She didn't have to, but she did."

Angel saw a moment of confusion ripple across Chris's face and she took the opening. "Do you think it's better if that sort of thing happens before a wedding or after?"

"That's your justification?" asked Chris. She took a step back and turned away from Angel. After a moment, the tension in her frame seemed to relax a little, signaling a change in her demeanor.

Angel eased her stance as well. "Come on, you're gay. You understand how somebody with deep questions about their sexuality may want to find some answers before a big commitment like—"

Chris spun around on her heel to face Angel again. "I'm not gay," she said, matter-of-factly.

Angel's eyebrows shot up in confusion now. "What?"

Chris shrugged, her hands in the air. "Not gay. Totally straight."

"Oh, s-sorry," stammered Angel, thinking about that blush, which just wouldn't have happened if Chris hadn't understood *exactly* what Angel had been thinking. Usually, straight girls were much too oblivious to figure something like that out that fast. "Thought I got a vibe, but—"

"Nope. I like dick. I really like it," Chris said with a big smile. "Look, I think we've gotten off on the wrong foot. If Maddie likes you, you can't be all bad."

Angel shook her head slightly, a little dizzy from the complete change in direction of the conversation. She took her own step back.

"Hey, how about I knock off here and we go get a drink. Boy, it is hot in here, isn't it? Woo! I could use a drink!" Chris smiled and dragged an arm across her damp brow. She darted over to the desk. "There's a little place a couple blocks from here. Would you like to try that?" And without waiting for a response, she added, "Just let me lock up my laptop."

With her back to Angel, she pulled a set of keys from her pocket. She closed the laptop and bent down to put it in a drawer, glanced back ever so briefly at Angel's eyes, and then bent down much lower and slower and leaned over much further than she needed to, to put the laptop away.

CHAPTER FIVE

"I knew the plan would work!"

Lucy did a fist pump in the air with her left hand while her right balanced a paper plate holding an open bratwurst bun. Mike was right behind her with two plates, one with a bun on it and one with two buns.

Chris manned the charcoal grill and flipped the sizzling brats onto the buns. The three of them went over to a patio table positioned on a large deck in the shade of a tall tree. The table was already set with ketchup, mustard, onions, and sauerkraut for the brats, fresh green beans from the farmers market, sliced strawberries, and deli potato salad.

"I don't know if it worked. I just asked her to join me for a couple of beers and she did." Chris took a big bite of her brat. "She didn't hit on me or anything."

Of course, Chris had been sweaty and dirty and wearing her steel-toed boots at a dive bar so it may have been a big ask to expect Angel to hit on her then. Although she had practically begged to be hit on after that humiliating move, bending over the desk to show off her "assets." She shook her head and closed her eyes, willing that memory out of her brain, but the memory remained.

"Yeah, but she asked you out to dinner. Isn't asking a girl out to dinner hitting on her?" Mike bunched up his brow in confusion as he continued to fix up his two brats. "When I ask a girl out to dinner, I'm usually hitting on her."

"I got the impression it was more of a reward for returning the phone," Chris said.

"Which I still haven't forgiven you for, by the way," Mike grumped.

"Forgive me? You can thank me for keeping you out of jail."

"Well, if she didn't invite you on a date then you just make it one anyway," interjected Lucy, happily drowning her brat in ketchup.

"What?" asked Chris.

"She's a lesbian. She asked you, a woman, to dinner. It's perfectly reasonable to think it's a date. So, you get all dressed up, do the makeup and the hair, and it's a date. Just like that."

"I have a new shirt. It has stripes. I could wear that with a nice pair of pants."

Lucy piled green beans onto her plate. "Your lesbian date clothes won't work. Remember? She has to think you're straight."

Chris groaned. "You know, it's time you restained this deck. I put a lot of time into building it and if you don't take care of it these decking boards will rot."

"You'll build me a new, even better one. No changing the subject. You'll come over here before the dinner. I've got stuff you can wear." Lucy grabbed her brat, ready to take a big bite. "No worries."

Mike nodded. "No worries."

Worries, thought Chris.

* * *

Lucy tapped a finger on her chin while scanning the items in her closet. "You're taller than me, but we're around the same size otherwise." Lucy poked through some hanging items. "No slacks. No sleeves. Too tall for that. Those broad shoulders are a problem, too."

Chris sat on the bed, dreading the entire operation.

"This should work." Lucy pulled a fire-engine red dress out of her closet and handed it to Chris. "Try this on. There's a full-length mirror behind the door if you want to look."

Lucy left the bedroom and shut the door to sit down in the living room with her brother.

"Hurry up! I wanna' see!" Mike called out.

After a few minutes Chris opened the door and stepped out of the room to present herself to the two on the couch. She marveled again at how, despite Lucy's petite size and Mike's massive frame they still were obviously siblings with identical ginger coloring and very similar facial features. Both were very fair-skinned, lightly freckled, with small noses and strong jaws, long fingers and arms and red hair that frizzed with the slightest bit of humidity. Humidity would leave Lucy with a wild red mane that surrounded her head like a fireball, while her brother, who was already starting to thin on top, was left with something a little more Bozo-esque.

Mike whistled. "Wow, Chris! I hardly ever see you in a dress."

Chris tugged on the sides of the dress. "It feels weird."

"That's knee length on me but just longer than a miniskirt on you. Otherwise, that fits perfectly!" said Lucy.

"From the front but look at the back. It's too tight." Chris turned around to show Mike and Lucy the red fabric straining across her bottom.

Lucy got up and walked over to inspect the situation more closely.

"It's tight." Lucy tugged at the seams of the dress. "But, actually, to really good effect. If you had an ounce of cellulite I'd say, 'Don't do it,' but on you it totally works."

"But my ass looks ridiculous!"

Mike tucked his tongue back in his mouth. "It's not ridiculous. Speaking as a man, I'd have to say it complements your figure nicely."

Lucy shook her head. "You can't wear those panties. They leave lines. Do you have a thong?"

"No."

"You can borrow one of mine."

"No!"

"You'll have to go commando then."

"NO!"

Fighting the confines of the dress, Chris struggled to stride over to a chair where Lucy had hung a sweater.

"Maybe with a sweater…" She reached for the long white sweater on the back of the chair. She threw it over her shoulders and looked back to see if it reached all the way down to her thighs.

Lucy took the sweater away. "No sweater."

Mike stuck his hand in the air. "I vote 'No sweater,' too."

Lucy put the sweater back on the chair.

Chris clasped her hands together in a plea. "Come on! My ass looks huge in this dress. This is a dumb plan. It'll never work."

Lucy just nodded. "Oh, it'll work all right. You just gotta flirt with her. You know, smile at her, compliment her, laugh at her jokes. Look at you in that dress. She'll have no clue. Just don't let her get too close. You exude dykiness—"

"Exude?"

"—and she'll immediately know you're not straight if you hug her or kiss her or, god forbid, sleep with her."

"Don't sleep with her!" Mike reiterated.

"Don't sleep with her!" repeated Lucy. "If you sleep with her, she'll know you're gay and she'll run straight back to Maddie."

Chris clapped her hands on her forehead in frustration. "There's an awful lot of assumptions to unpack in that."

"Boy, if you slept with her that would really be a betrayal. My fiancée and my best friend," Mike added.

"The ultimate betrayal," said Lucy.

Chris shook her head. "I'm NOT going to sleep with her. And it's a dumb plan."

"It's not a dumb plan. Just a crazy, desperate plan." Lucy put an arm around Mike's shoulders. "But Mike is a crazy, desperate man."

"So desperate," Mike added with big, sad eyes.

Lucy's phone rang. She pulled it out of her pocket and checked the screen.

"I gotta take this," she said leaving the room.

Mike looked at the sneakers on Chris's feet. "Do you have a pair of shoes to wear with that or are you going to wear a pair of Lucy's?"

Chris grabbed the sides of the dress and started yanking on it hard to get it to go down as far as possible. "Yeah, I have a pair that would work that I haven't worn in a long time. I don't know why I never wear them. I do put on a dress occasionally. But I still don't think I want to do this—"

Lucy walked back into the room, looking grim.

Chris looked at Lucy in concern. "What is it? What's wrong?"

Lucy took a big breath and then went to sit down next to her brother. She took his hand. "Maddie has decided that you should hold off on making the final payment for the wedding venue."

Mike's mouth flopped open for a second. "But we'll lose the venue!"

Chris and Lucy held their breath while they let that sink in. And then Mike's face contorted into a look of pure agony, and he started wailing into his sister's shoulder. As she patted his head and rubbed his back, Lucy threw Chris a serious look and Chris threw her hands up in surrender.

CHAPTER SIX

So, is it a date? Or not a date? Angel contemplated that thought as she sipped on a glass of ice water at a table in the busy restaurant. She was surprised to find herself in this situation, as her intention had been simply to get her phone and get away. Instead, Chris had asked about going someplace close for a beer together. In her head Angel had responded, "Thanks, no, I gotta go," but out of her mouth came, "Yeah, I'd love a beer." Damn, that woman had looked so good bent over the desk! Angel took another sip of her water.

They had walked a few blocks to a local tavern, not much more than a hole in the wall with a couple of taps and some blue-collar guys who had knocked off early from jobs in the industrial park. It wasn't the typical sort of place Angel would hang out or even go into, but Chris had looked comfortable enough with her hair pulled up in a ponytail and her steel-toed boots.

Lesbian. Definitely lesbian, Angel had thought as they sat at a sticky table and drank their pints. But her boyfriend, a fiancé no less, was the first thing Chris had started talking about. His name was David and he traveled a lot for work, electrical substation construction or something like that. Chris had assured Angel that she loved him a lot, even though he was currently on a job that would have him away for a few months.

"Engaged?" Angel had said. She popped a glance at Chris's bare left ring finger and Chris quickly tucked her hand under the table.

"Well, not officially. Not yet. But we are getting married. I know it."

"Does David know it?"

With extreme satisfaction, Angel watched that blush climb up Chris's throat again. Why did she find it so entertaining to get a rise out of the woman? Fortunately, that was all Chris said about him for the rest of that afternoon; they drank their beers and mostly talked about work stuff.

Chris had mentioned that she had just started the new business with her partner Mike and Angel had mentioned that she had been running various small businesses for years. They talked for a while about the pros and cons of subcontracting versus hiring employees. Chris had no experience hiring employees, but she and Mike had already had some jobs where they could have used help. Angel had plenty of experience with hiring, so Chris had asked a lot of questions about tax reporting requirements, employment eligibility verification steps, and liability insurance. In solidarity with another female small business owner Angel had been happy to answer Chris's business questions. It was payback for all the women who had mentored Angel over the years.

Maddie and Mike hadn't come up as a topic at all, which Angel was grateful for but had been rather surprised about. Clearly, Chris had been avoiding the topic. It had occurred to her that Chris may have just been trying to learn more about this interloper, herself, in Mike and Maddie's relationship. Keep your friends close and your enemies closer, as it were.

Angel sighed as thoughts of Maddie came into her head. Things had pretty much gone exactly as planned with her.

Angel had noticed the reserved Maddie at the strip club out on some sort of girls' night with the crazy, petite ginger. The little redhead looked like trouble, but Angel had noticed Maddie noticing her. That was Angel's method of operation. Hang out at the bar and notice the women who couldn't stop looking at her despite the male strippers on the stage. With her short hair and her ability to move with a masculine swagger when wearing denim or leather or other clothes straight women stereotypically thought gay women wore, she could easily communicate her sexual preference to other women. Then all she had to do was tune into who was watching her.

At a lesbian bar or a Tegan and Sara concert a lesbian would immediately have hit on her. After a few romps in bed the woman would be interested in getting the U-Haul packed and the dog interviewed for enrollment at a doggie daycare close to Angel's home. Yeah, in her experience that wasn't an inaccurate stereotype at all. So it was the straight women who just wanted to experiment that Angel was really interested in. Even better if they had a partner they didn't want to find out about that. When their lesbian fling was over, they could run straight back to the warm, loving arms of their husbands or boyfriends, no worse for the wear. Some may have gotten a little too attached, but as soon as it came to Angel's attention, she would end it.

"It's not you, it's me."

Well, that was true, anyway. Holding a woman, touching her, tasting her; Angel wanted that. *Needed* that. But a new relationship? No. One turn-you-inside-out, leave-your-guts-on-the-floor devastation in a lifetime was enough for her.

So randy women uninterested in, or unavailable for, a relationship were what she sought out. The place she often found them was at the male review on ladies' night at the local gay club.

Maddie had fit the bill perfectly, and after securing an introduction via the redhead, Maddie had accepted the invitation to her bed that night. Usually, all the straight women wanted was a taste. After finally experiencing sex with a lover who knew what a clit was, where it was located, and what to do with it, they would leave very satisfied, and Angel would never hear from them again. Sometimes, though, they would call back one, two, maybe several times before they got it completely out of their systems, and Angel was happy to oblige. Maddie had been one of those.

Of course, the husbands and boyfriends were never supposed to find out. In Maddie's case her fiancé had found out before Maddie had been able to determine if she liked sex better with women and it was making for a lot of drama.

Angel made a mental note to call Maddie and see how she was doing. She had been talking about delaying or even canceling the wedding, and if she had done something like that she was sure to be distraught.

Angel blew air through her lips in frustration and shoved her water glass around the table. This time her fling *had* been left worse for the wear and that wasn't what Angel had intended. She didn't really want to be involved in the problems between Maddie and Mike, but she felt like she had been responsible for a car accident and needed to stay and render aid to the victims rather than leave the scene of the accident like a coward.

How Chris fit into the entire mix was a mystery to Angel. After the pints at the bar with Chris, Angel had sent Maddie a quick text asking about who Mike worked with. She didn't get much back except to learn they were friends and business partners. Angel had wanted to ask Maddie what she knew about Chris's relationship status, but asking questions of the person you are currently sleeping with about the sexual habits of somebody you'd like to sleep with was, in Angel's experience, unwise, so she let it drop at that.

Was that why she had invited Chris out to dinner? Was she hoping to sleep with her? She had offered to buy Chris dinner as a reward for returning the phone after she had turned down a cash reward at the bar. Angel had enjoyed her company immensely and didn't want to never see her again. Chris had been tense and awkward when they first got to the bar, but after the pint started to work its magic and Chris started to loosen up, they began talking like they were old friends instead of the practical strangers they really were.

Chris laughed easily and was clearly smart and committed to her business, and she had been adorable in the sweaty, dirty tank top and beat-up work boots and the way she got all excited when she started talking about dovetail joints, of all things. You could have knocked Angel over with a feather when Chris told her she was straight. She knew plenty of very feminine gay women who defied their stereotype, though, and she knew the same could go for straight women, too. So that Chris was straight was certainly within the realm of possibility. Maybe this dinner out was just a transactional reward for the return of the phone. Or maybe, given the neglectful boyfriend off building power substations out in the wilderness somewhere, it was a date. It was all rather confusing. Whatever it was, she was just grateful Chris had agreed to join her. In the short time they had known each other, she had felt a connection with Chris that she hadn't been able to bear making with another woman in years. She really didn't want that to slip away so fast.

Angel took another sip from her water glass and checked the time on her phone. It was just a couple of minutes before the time they had agreed to meet at the restaurant. Chris wasn't late yet.

* * *

Chris checked the time on her phone. A couple of minutes until she was late. But that was the plan. Lucy's plan, of course. Lucy had tried to explain to her why it was important to be a little late for this dinner with Angel, but the reasoning escaped her. At Lucy's insistence she had agreed to show up late, but late wasn't her style and her tardiness for dinner was making her uncomfortable. But not as uncomfortable as the damn borrowed thong she was wearing. She squirmed in the back seat of the Uber.

She had already known that women were idiots for wearing high heels, like the ankle-breakers she had on right now. But now she also knew that women were idiots for wearing thongs. Again, at Lucy's insistence, Chris had agreed to wear one. But, of course, her butt and hips were much bigger than Lucy's.

She had been able to get it on. Sure, it bit, but she figured the thing would eventually stretch out as it was forced to conform to the shape of her ass. The distortion would likely be permanent, but she had no intention of returning the thong anyway. She had been seriously wrong about that theory, unfortunately, and in the back seat of the Uber the small, resilient bit of fabric was operating like a vise clamped to her privates.

She squirmed as with every bounce of the Uber across a city pothole, and there were plenty, the too-small red thong brutally chafed her most sensitive bits. It had to be pulled loose.

She stuffed her phone back in her clutch purse. There wasn't enough slack in the front of the dress to get a hold of the thong, and she wanted to avoid reaching clear under the dress in a stranger's car. She pulled slack the seat belt across her shoulder and leaned over to try to grab the thong from the rear, but there was no way to get a purchase on it through the sausage casing of a dress which was already straining its limits of structural integrity. Catastrophic seam failure loomed as a real possibility; she was afraid to put too much pressure on the material.

As she struggled to grasp the medieval torture device crammed up her buttcrack, she noticed the Uber driver looking at her in the rearview mirror, his eyebrows up around his hairline. She sat back in the seat and released the seat belt to allow it to go back into tension against her chest. She decided she'd take the thong off at the restaurant as soon as she got there. Otherwise, by the end of the night the damn thing would be crammed so far up her lady parts she would need needle-nose pliers to remove it and she didn't have her toolbox.

* * *

Angel nodded at the waitstaff who offered to refill her water glass and checked the time on her phone again. Late. Angel had already sent Chris a couple of texts. *I have a table for us near the back*, and, *Let me know if you need directions.* And Angel had received a couple of texts in return reading, *On my way!* and *Guess I'm late*, with an *Oops!* emoji.

Angel hated being played in the stupid waiting game. For somebody else she might have considered just walking out, but for some reason unknown to her she really wanted to see this woman again. She snorted into her glass at the thought of it.

Then she saw a beautiful young woman walk into the dining room and step up to the vacant host stand. She went breathless and gasped out loud when she realized it was Chris. At the bar she had sported a ponytail, dirty tank, and ass-kicker boots. Now her honey-highlighted brown locks were loose and wavy on her shoulders. Fire-engine red lipstick matched the killer red dress she was wearing. Angel watched as she stumbled a little bit in the heels, clearly not used to them, and then did a one-eighty turn to peer around the dining room and then the bar and then the hallway past the bar. As Chris stood on tiptoes to see over the crowd, her back to the dining room, Angel's eyelids lowered heavily at the sight of the taut red fabric of the dress straining to contain her generous bottom.

"Daaaamn!" Angel groaned quietly to herself with a tone that seeped up from deep in her chest. So, this *was* a date. She reached up and opened two more buttons on her blouse and looked down to check to make sure the expensive bra was doing its job. It was.

Angel stood up at the table, then put her hand in the air to get Chris's attention. She watched as she did another pivot to face the dining room again. She grew concerned at the pained expression she saw on Chris's face. Worried that she was becoming frustrated at not being able to find their table, she quickly headed over to her.

Chris was trying to get her shoe heel back under her foot when Angel arrived at her side and reached out to grab her elbow. Startled, Chris spun around and teetered a bit more despite Angel stepping closer to grab the other elbow. Angel watched as her eyes bounced down to the generous cleavage she had on display and then immediately back up to her eyes. Watching her chest heave as she forgot to breathe, Angel decided the bra had been worth the money.

Angel smiled. "Hi," she said in a relaxed, low voice, trying to calm Chris down a bit. The word came out sexier than she intended. She felt Chris shiver in her hands.

"Hi," Chris croaked after finally taking a breath.

"I have a table for us over there." Angel gestured toward the dining room, using her chin since she now had one hand on Chris's elbow and the other at her waist.

"Oh, gr-great!" Chris stammered.

Angel realized that Chris was flustered at their closeness. But she didn't ease up. Served the woman right for keeping her waiting.

"But I'd like to use the restroom before we sit down. Could you point me—"

"I'll take you." With that she put her hand on the back of Chris's bare, well-muscled upper arm and began escorting her to the hallway past the bar. Although Chris had a couple inches on Angel in the taller heels and she was definitely more muscular than Angel, she let herself be led to the restroom.

Once inside, Chris made a beeline for the oversized stall in the back. Angel went to wash her hands.

"Did you have any trouble finding the place?" Angel lathered her hands thickly. "Their website isn't quite up yet, so I was a little worried you'd have a hard time with the location."

"No...I...the Uber driver didn't have any trouble finding the street address."

Angel turned, curious at the sound of Chris's heels clattering on the floor of the stall. Obviously, she wasn't sitting, which made Angel wonder what was going on in there.

"It's a new place." Angel turned back to the sink and rinsed off her hands, admiring the chrome fixtures and the quartz countertop before heading over to the towel dispenser. Spotless. A clean bathroom practically ensured a clean kitchen. Her years in the industry had taught her that it was wise to check the bathroom before eating at any restaurant. "They're just open a couple nights a week now. They will have their grand opening in a few days." She checked her lipstick in the mirror.

"Really? Gosh, I never even heard of them. How did you find out about this place?"

Chris exited the stall. She appeared to be trying to conceal something behind her back.

"A couple of my former staff started this restaurant, so I wanted to see how they were doing."

Chris joined Angel by the towel dispenser, still holding something behind her back.

"Your staff? Are you...? Do you have a...? You mentioned your business was in food service when we went out for beers, but you never got more specific."

"Just a little French restaurant down—" As Angel turned to face the general direction of her restaurant, she heard Chris jam something quickly in the garbage can. When Angel turned back to face her, Chris smiled sweetly, her hands empty now. "Downtown near the capitol. Not much."

Chris hurried over to the sink and washed her hands quickly.

"Wow! Your own restaurant? I didn't know that."

Angel brought over a couple of hand towels and Chris accepted them with a grateful smile. She already seemed much more relaxed.

"Just a small business. It's a lot of work. But you know what that's like."

"I do." Chris chucked the towels in the garbage on top of whatever she had thrown in there earlier.

Angel looked at Chris and paused for a moment. "Feel better?"

She took a big breath and smiled. "Immensely!"

Angel smiled back. "Great! Then let's go get dinner."

CHAPTER SEVEN

Chris felt Angel's hand drift to her waist as they walked to the dining room. When they got there, she extended her arm to offer an escort to their table.

Chris side-eyed Angel's graciously extended bent elbow. Angel seemed perfectly comfortable offering an escort to a woman as if she, Angel, were a gentleman. And straight women probably took her arm all the time. But it wasn't Chris's habit to accept help to simply walk. Then again, nor was it her habit to wear ridiculous shoes that made merely walking safely impossible. Chris flashed to an image of herself striding on her own into the dining room, tripping on the maddening heels, tumbling ass over teakettle, and winding up with her dress balled up like a red belt around her waist, exposing her panty-free rear end to the entire dining crowd.

She blew a honey-blond lock out of her face and reached out to clamp on to Angel's arm. As they walked toward their table, she made a mental note to throw the heels in the trash as soon as she got home.

At their table Angel seated herself while the waiter held the chair for Chris. Chris sat down very, very carefully. Never in her life had she gone without underwear in public before, much less while wearing a skimpy, sexy dress. The initial relief of getting the thong off immediately turned into nervousness that she would be unable to keep her knees clamped together the entire night and would end up flashing some unfortunate soul who was just trying to eat dinner.

She started to relax as Angel ordered their drinks and they immediately picked up the conversation they had started at the tavern, discussing the ins and outs of small business operations, moving on to the topics of the foodie culture in town and a bit about local politics.

As Angel studied the menu, Chris took a moment to study her. The well-tailored sand-colored linen jacket she wore over a powder-blue blouse was buttoned low enough that she had to struggle hard to keep her gaze from being pulled in that direction. The fingers that were holding the menu were long and fine, the nails tightly trimmed and unpainted. A cropped haircut accentuated the pixie-ish point of her chin. She had full lips and straight, white teeth and highly expressive, steeply arched eyebrows that telegraphed every thought she was willing to share. Her right eyebrow, barely visible in the yellow candlelight from the table, had a white scar that cut horizontally through the top arch, lightly separating the top of the brow from the rest.

Angel glanced up from the menu for a moment at Chris. Her thickly lashed eyes, that in the fluorescent light of the bathroom had been a bright azure, now, in the light from the candle, were a darker shade of ultramarine.

A smile ticked up on the corner of Angel's mouth and she blinked. Chris quickly looked away, realizing she had been staring.

"I'm having the special," Angel said. "How about you?"

Dinner was marvelous. They both started with a wonderful mixed greens salad with radish, cucumber, and a slightly sweet champagne vinaigrette. For her main course Chris ordered prawns with sweet potato and a relish of coconut, pineapple, and chopped peanuts. Angel had the chicken confit with butternut squash, cipollini, and brussels sprouts in a maple glaze. They topped it all off with a perfect, crisp, dry white wine Angel picked out. It was all delicious, and Chris ate every last bite. She was thankful that the dress at least had some give in the waist because she needed the extra room.

After the meal, the head chef came to their table. Angel stood up for a hug and the two clapped each other jovially on the back and talked like long-lost friends. Angel called him Chef John. When Angel introduced Chris to him, he complimented Angel on her lovely date. Chris felt her face blush hard. Lucy had been right about how to turn a dinner between new acquaintances into a date.

The chef inquired after the meal and Chris sincerely raved about the food while Angel good naturedly teased about the rough competition he was providing.

"You two haven't had dessert yet!" said John while the empty plates were cleared from the table. "Try the lingonberry sour cream pie. You'll love it!"

The chef waved more staff over and promptly a piece of pie appeared on the table with two forks.

"Angel," said John, "I would love for you to see the kitchen after the dinner crush slows down. Think you could stop by the bar for some drinks and then come to the back of the house later? Your night is on me."

Angel and Chris grinned at the chef, and Angel graciously accepted the offer. He went back to the kitchen and, despite both being stuffed to the gills, Angel and Chris dug into the pie. It had a bright red lingonberry filling the color of Chris's dress, a mid-layer of creamy, white sour cream custard, and a topping of delicious brown sugar and hazelnut crumble that sweetened the entire dessert just the right amount.

Angel turned to Chris, her eyes glinting in the light from the candle. "Okay if we stick around and hang out on the patio for a while?"

A sincere smile crossed Chris's face. "I'd love that."

Chris was starting to feel a little tipsy. She was a lightweight and knew she should be careful about drinks from the bar. But it had been forever since she had been on a date, and even longer since she had been on an enjoyable one, so she decided to go ahead and have a few more drinks. Hadn't she taken the Uber instead of driving herself for just this possibility?

Besides, the reason she was here was so Angel could forget about Maddie and pursue her instead, right? So, better if Angel had a couple of drinks and got more relaxed herself. Maybe Chris could lure Angel's affections from Maddie to herself if she could get Angel a little drunk.

The evening was warm and humid, and an orange moon was out over the cozy patio. The space was decorated with string lights and high tables and chairs and a few low, comfortable chairs in the back in pods around short coffee tables.

At the bar off the patio Chris ordered an Aperol Spritz and Angel ordered a Manhattan.

"Shall we sit down in the corner where we can be a little more comfortable?" Angel asked, gesturing to a couple of the cushy, low chairs that were unoccupied.

Chris smiled and nodded, and they headed over.

"I love a good patio," said Angel. "I've got plans to install a rooftop patio at my restaurant. Well, sometimes they seem more like dreams than plans."

Soon enough they were once again rapt in a conversation about the joys and perils of small business ownership.

"Get a good CPA," seemed to be Angel's main piece of hard-learned advice. "Don't try to do that yourself. A good CPA is worth their weight in gold."

But it turned out they also both had a fondness for travel, and books, and food—Chris, eating, and Angel, cooking—and the conversation just kept going.

Angel, with her jacket off and the sleeves of her blouse rolled up, was slowly sipping her first Manhattan and Chris was on her second (or third?) spritzer, when Angel made Chris laugh so hard, describing her own personal lesson regarding why you never joke with TSA about a concealed weapon in your bra, that a little spritzer came out of Chris's nose. Chris leaned forward so quickly to grab a napkin on the table to put to her face that she completely lost track of her knees.

"You know what?" said Angel, "I'd love to have a view of the bar and see how the foot traffic moves around the patio. Do you mind if we switch sides and you can sit here and face the corner while I sit there where I can see everybody? Is that okay with you?"

"Sure!" Chris said, setting her almost empty glass on the other side of the table. She scooched forward a little bit for better leverage to get out of the low chair, grateful when Angel grabbed her hands to give her a boost. They were trying to navigate around each other between the chairs when Chris, a little wobbly from the shoes and booze, suddenly found herself in Angel's arms.

Chris giggled an apology, but Angel did not let go right away. Instead, with Chris in her arms, Angel's gaze traveled to her throat, down her shoulder, and then to the cleavage above Chris's dress, and then slowly up to her ear. Angel leaned in. Her skin smelled like cedar and orange. She put her cheek against Chris's and softly spoke, her warm breath moving past Chris's ear. "It's been my experience that women who go out wearing sexy fire-engine red dresses and no panties are really just interested in getting well laid. So how about we get out of here and go back to my apartment?"

Crap! Chris froze, appalled that she had forgotten she wasn't wearing underwear and that Angel had figured it out.

"Please." Angel moved her hand up Chris's back and began caressing her shoulder gently.

A sudden, unexpected battle erupted inside of Chris, with her body screaming, *Yes, yes!* and her brain saying, *No, remember the plan!*

Fuck the plan! was her body's reply.

Angel drew in a deep breath, her nose in Chris's neck, and then Chris leaned out, pushing Angel away and stepping back.

"Gosh, I've never seen a working kitchen before." Chris ran a clawed hand through her hair, attempting to gather her wits. "I was kind of looking forward to that."

Angel paused for a moment. Confusion crossed her face, and she too wobbled a bit, like she was trying to get her bearings. Then she straightened up and smiled. "Absolutely." She peered around at the crowd. "The height of the dinner rush is over. Let's see if they'll let us in the kitchen now."

In short order they were in the back of the house for a tour. Angel and Chef John were immediately engrossed in conversation about staffing and kitchen layout and table revenue and several other issues Chris couldn't hope to follow. So, while they talked she took in the cacophony of sights and sounds and smells around her; the meats searing, soups bubbling, pots and lids clashing, knives thumping on chopping blocks, and people yelling orders around the room.

If it was a little warm and humid on the patio, it felt like a sauna in the kitchen. Yet, despite the heat, the staff rushed back and forth through the space, carrying this, hoisting that, pounding some other thing. And although Chris had been assured that the dinner rush was mostly over, it still looked like complete chaos to her.

John was pulled away by the sound of a crashing pot in the back and Chris turned to Angel. "Wow! It's crazy here. Is this what your kitchen is like?"

"Would you like to see it?"

Chris hesitated. There was something almost irresistible about this woman. But she *had* resisted. She had turned down the invitation to Angel's apartment, as surprisingly difficult as that had been. Clearly, she could keep her head around Angel, so...

"I'd really like for you to see my restaurant." Angel looked at her with warm, expectant eyes.

She smiled and nodded. "I'd love to."

Soon Chris and Angel were speeding away in Angel's sleek, low Audi. With its spotless interior, quiet engine, and smooth ride, it was a far cry from what she drove, a beat-up Subaru Forester pushing two hundred thousand miles and filled in the back with random tools. She made a mental note to make sure Angel didn't see her very lesbian car.

"Nice car," said Chris, stroking the smooth dash. "You must be killing it at the restaurant business."

"I do okay."

"Beautiful, charming, successful. You must have a lot of women who want to spend time with you."

Angel gave Chris a sidelong smile. "I do okay," she repeated.

"So, are you and Maddie serious?" Chris asked awkwardly. "I mean, she's still engaged to Mike as far as we know so it can't be that serious, but...I was wondering if..."

"I'm not in an exclusive relationship right now, if that's what you're asking."

"I see," Chris replied shyly, looking at her hands in her lap.

"How about you?" asked Angel, smoothly navigating the car through a complicated intersection. "You mentioned a boyfriend, a fiancé, but are you exclusive?"

"Of course," Chris replied, confused by the question. She assumed having a fiancé sort of implied exclusivity. Although, given the mess with Maddie and Angel's reputation in general, maybe she needed to make a distinction between intended exclusivity and actual practice.

Angel confidently steered the car into a parking space off the pedestrian mall of State Street, which only allowed limited vehicular traffic of buses, cabs, and emergency vehicles. "We're just around the corner."

She parked the car and jumped out. Chris opened her car door and Angel was there to take her hand.

"They'll be closing up soon. Come on."

Chris got out of the car and the two walked down the block, Chris's arm through Angel's for balance. They walked around the corner and onto State Street, which was buzzing with barhoppers walking and biking up and down the well-lit street from the stately Madison capitol building at the top of the street to the busy University of Wisconsin campus on the bottom. Along the historic street were small, squat one-, two-, and three-story buildings. Angel stopped them in front of one of them.

Chris looked up at the sign over the door. "Wow! You own Olivia's Café?"

Angel grinned at Chris. Far from being a little French cuisine restaurant near the capitol, Olivia's was one of the trendiest restaurants in town. When they entered, Angel was immediately greeted by the staff. Despite the impending close the place was still reasonably busy with around a third of the tables occupied.

The building interior was beautiful, a converted industrial space with exposed brick and wood and steel beam trusses across the ceiling. In contrast to the heavy factory walls and structure, the dining room was lit with delicate chandeliers with many fine, twinkling crystals. White tablecloths covered tables set with black napkins on white china. Staff were busy at a long, well-stocked bar in the back, and a bank of windows on one end of the dining room looked out at the foot traffic on the street.

"The kitchen is this way," Angel said to Chris, grinning, clearly proud of the operation. She took her hand and led her to the back.

The kitchen was starting to wind down. Staff were cleaning the workstations and equipment while a poor man labored away at cleaning a mountain of dishes. Angel introduced Chris as a friend to the staff and started chatting with them regarding how the evening dinner service had gone.

"Feel free to look around," Angel told Chris, and she began to assess the cabinets and drawers, opening a few to examine the hinges, latches, glides, slides, and runners. She narrowed her eyes at the seams of one countertop which was gapped just on the bare side of acceptable. Past the sink and the freezers, she watched a couple of staff take a mysterious staircase up to a second floor and disappear around a turn. She glanced at Angel, who was busy in a conversation with her staff. She looked up the staircase and decided to go up.

CHAPTER EIGHT

A door at the top of the staircase was cracked open, allowing the cool night breeze to tumble into the stairway. She pushed the door open. A couple of staff were sitting on some stacked decking boards piled next to the door, relaxing while they smoked cigarettes, the gray swirls of smoke rising over their heads into the night sky.

Chris put the toe of her shoe on the rooftop surface and gave it a little dig. A high quality EPMD rubber membrane had been installed. Extremely durable to weather and UV exposure but not invulnerable to a pair of heels. She took her shoes off and carried them in her hand as she walked across the space lit only by a bare bulb over the door and the waxing moon overhead.

Long boards were scattered about, along with a large pile of stacked aluminum joists. There was even an abandoned wheelbarrow. Clearly, it was a site under construction and walking across it barefoot in the dark probably wasn't the smartest idea. But the lights on the buildings around her and sounds of the city below drew Chris to the edge of the roof, which was protected with a four-foot wall. She put her hands on the wall and peered over the edge to the alley below and the rooftops of the small shops and houses beyond Olivia's. Off in the distance she could see moonlight glinting off the northern city lake, Lake Mendota.

"Come see the other side."

Chris startled at Angel's voice immediately behind her and spun around. Angel was holding out her hand.

"Come on."

Chris took her hand.

"Be careful. There is a lot of construction stuff around."

Chris carefully stepped over a board, hanging on to Angel's hand for balance.

"Is this your dream rooftop patio?" Chris asked.

"Yes." Angel pointed in one direction. "Two- and four-top tables that can be pushed together for larger groups. A small bar over there for events." She pointed another way. "This stairway goes down to the kitchen, but there is a second stairway over there that goes down to the entrance for customers. That's the dream. Though it's more like a nightmare now that the contractor quit on me."

"Who's the contractor?"

Angel gave her a name. Chris nodded. His reputation in the city for being unreliable was well deserved.

They made their way to the other side of the rooftop, and Chris put her hands on top of the wall and peered over to see the trendy pedestrian- and bikeway below.

"Look up the street," said Angel.

Chris leaned over the wall and got a glimpse of the stunning, illuminated white dome topped with a gold figure against the black night sky. "Look at how pretty the capitol is from here. You'll have the most romantic restaurant in the city when you get this done."

Angel put a hand on Chris's waist. She glanced at the stack of decking boards by the door, but the staff had already finished their cigarettes and had gone back inside.

"Who's Olivia?"

Angel paused and then took a deep breath. "She was my inspiration for the restaurant."

She appeared to shrug something off, and then she took a step to stand close in front of Chris. Her fair complexion was strongly shadowed in the moonlight, and her gracefully arched eyebrows were set with resolve. In the dim light, Chris could just see the white scar through Angel's brow and the tuft of hair that curled in rebellion above the eyebrow line over the scar.

Rambunctious college kids howled on the street below and a car beeped in annoyance at a nearby intersection. The sounds on the street echoed off the pavement and buildings before arriving, muted, on the rooftop where they stood. Smells from the kitchen wafted past them on the cooling, damp, night air.

Angel stepped closer.

Keep your head! Keep your head! Chris reminded herself. "My boyfriend, ah, David—"

"Let's not talk about him." Angel put her arms around Chris's waist and drew her close.

"If you're going to kiss me, I have to remind you that I'm straight." Chris's voice trembled slightly.

"Yeah. You told me." Angel moved her lips closer to hers.

Chris closed her eyes and held her breath in anticipation of the kiss. She could feel the heat of Angel's breath on her mouth, and her hips pressed into Angel's of their own accord.

"I can't kiss you. I can't kiss you." Chris dropped her shoes and purse on the rubber-coated roof. Her voice was weak, and her knees felt like they might buckle. Nothing happened. When Chris opened her eyes, she saw Angel watching her with some concern.

"What are you waiting for?" Chris wrapped her fingers in the short, dark curls that fringed Angel's head and held her for a moment before pulling Angel in for a gentle kiss.

Angel's lips were soft and warm and lightly wet against Chris's mouth, and her hair was silky and pliant in her fingers.

She pulled back to gauge Angel's reaction. Angel smiled and leaned back in. They kissed again, more deeply this time. Angel opened her mouth and as Chris matched the movement an involuntary whimper rose from her chest. Angel pulled her tighter and gently slipped her tongue past Chris's lips. Hesitatingly, Chris lifted her tongue to meet hers.

The instant she tasted Angel's tongue, Chris pulled away, trying to catch her breath, which was coming in quick pants. Her heart was pounding in her chest. Butterflies were doing a rumba in her stomach. Angel leaned in and kissed her neck under her ear and the city lights swirled in her vision. Her head swam and her knees went weak. Holding her up, Angel returned to Chris's mouth and kissed her deeper still. Their tongues connected again. This time Angel groaned. Their kisses grew more fevered with Chris pressing her mouth hard into Angel's and clutching at her shirt while Angel met Chris's pressure with her own and drove her hands up and down her back.

Angel's hands went lower, and she pushed the dress up over Chris's bare hips. She worked her hand between her thighs. "Is it okay—"

"Yes."

"—if I—"

"Yes."

"—touch—"

"Yes!"

Startled by loud laughing from the staff pounding up the stairs, headed for the rooftop, both pulled back. Chris yanked her dress down, and Angel patted down her curls. Chris felt for her heels and purse on the dark roof next to her and snatched them up. They watched as the staff burst through the door to the rooftop and grabbed spaces to sit on the stacked boards.

Chris turned back to Angel and looked intently into her still smoldering gaze. "Does your restaurant have a room with a locking door?"

In less than a minute Angel had navigated them down the stairs and through the kitchen, sneaking past a couple of busy staff there, to a small office off the pantry. She flipped on a light while Chris went inside and dropped her purse and shoes in the corner. Chris heard the click of the latch as Angel spun the thumb-turn on the handle to lock the door.

Inside the bare office was a flimsy IKEA-style desk with a few papers and a phone on top. In front of it was a wheeled chair and next to it was a filing cabinet with a printer. In the corner sat a small safe. Muffled voices and the muted clatter of silverware emanated from the dining room just beyond the thin office wall.

Chris turned to face Angel, who was still by the door. Her heart pounded and her ears began to roar. She beckoned Angel over. Angel hurried to stand close to her, and Chris reached up and began unbuttoning her blouse. Her fingers shook and she fumbled with the buttons in her rush.

A laugh in the dining room on the other side of the wall was followed by some loud conversation and the clinking of dishes being cleared. Chris and Angel paused for a moment at the sound.

Angel looked intently at Chris, her gaze sharpened by passion. "Can you be quiet?"

Chris smiled and licked her lips. "Can you?"

Angel grabbed the papers and phone on the desk and dropped them on the file cabinet. Chris hopped on the desktop and Angel stood in front of her. She wrapped her legs around Angel's hips, her red dress riding up to expose her womanly center.

Angel kissed her mouth deeply and ran her hands up and down her bare thighs. Chris reached under her open shirt and around to the back, where she fumbled with the clasp on her bra until it was undone. Angel backed up a moment to pull off her blouse and bra, which she tossed over the printer. Chris's eyes dropped to her round, high, full breasts, and she smiled. She looked back up into Angel's eyes and opened her legs wider. Angel grinned at the invitation.

Angel stepped back and got down on her knees. She leaned forward to bury her face between Chris's legs, her searching tongue immediately finding its target. Chris let out a small, choked squeal, biting her lip to stay quiet, then threw her head back and squirmed as Angel got to work. Angel reached up and grabbed her hips to hold her steady while her tongue pursued its mission.

Chris's breaths came in quick gasps with irrepressible moans escaping her throat.

Angel switched out her tongue with her fingers.

"Shh. Shh," Chris heard off in the distance somewhere as she gradually ascended, several times thinking she had reached the peak only to climb still higher. Angel hopped on the desk and pressed her lips hard into Chris's, and Chris heard her own voice muffled in Angel's mouth. As she was reaching her goal, like a climber stretching out to put a hand on the rock that marked the apex of the mountain, a niggling thought needled its way up through the fog in her brain. She pulled her face away from Angel and pried her eyes open to see an intense look of concentration on Angel's face.

"The desk..." Chris panted. "...it can't—"

A wisp of confusion crossed Angel's face, and then, with an enormous, echoing *"CRACK!"* the desk broke in half in an explosion of laminate and particle board. Chris and Angel came crashing to the floor with the splintered desk. The desk chair spun away to slam into the opposite wall with a huge bang. Somebody in the dining room yelled in surprise.

Chris, once again, broke Angel's fall.

Angel pushed herself up on her hands, off Chris. "Oh, god! Are you okay?"

Somebody banged loudly on the door.

"Is somebody in there?" came an urgent male voice from the other side of the door. The doorknob rattled loudly as he attempted to get it open.

"C...can't...breathe!" Chris gasped.

Angel jumped to her feet. "You got the wind knocked out of you again."

Chris made a strangled sound, panic swirling around in her brain at the lack of oxygen.

There was more insistent pounding at the door. "Who's in there?"

Angel snatched her blouse off the printer and jerked it on. She jammed her bra in her pocket and quickly started to do the buttons on the shirt.

"It's okay, Jasper!" Angel called toward the door. "Just me! I dropped something."

Chris made a strangled wheezing sound as she fought to draw air into her chest.

"Breathe," Angel told her. "Breathe."

"Dropped something? A grenade? Angel! Are you okay? Open the door."

The door handle rattled again.

Angel pulled Chris to her feet and frantically yanked Chris's dress down from around her hips to back around her thighs while Chris steadied herself with a hand on the file cabinet. Then she ran to the door and put a hand on the rattling doorknob. Chris bent over, her hands on her knees and her mouth open as she gasped for air. Angel waited for a moment until Chris took a couple of good breaths.

"Angel? Is everything okay?" said another voice behind the door.

Chris lifted one hand and waved to Angel, signaling her recovery. Angel nodded, opened the door, and stepped out, quickly slamming the door shut behind her. Chris could hear muffled conversation on the other side of the door.

"What happened?" asked the male voice.

"I dropped a pen under the desk, and when I leaned on it to pick it up the desk broke," Angel said.

"The desk broke?"

"Piece of crap."

"Why was the door locked?" asked a female voice.

"Jo, make sure the temperature alarm is set on the walk-in."

"Just did."

Chris heard the conversation moving away from the door. She grabbed her purse, tugged her dress down a little lower, smoothed her hair down, and walked over to put her ear to the door.

"Nobody got hurt, did they?"

Nobody? So. The staff already knew Angel had not been alone in the office. Chris was overtaken by an overwhelming need to escape the building. She grabbed the door handle and wrenched the door open.

Angel was standing between two cooks, a lanky man with a goatee and a short, round woman with a butch haircut. All three turned around to look at Chris in surprise. The short cook gave Angel a knowing glance and started to snigger.

"Jo!" Angel barked at her. The sniggering stopped. Angel scowled and grabbed Jo and Jasper and started dragging them toward the kitchen. "Everybody is fine. Get back to work."

Chris grabbed her phone out of her purse and ran for the entrance. She navigated to her Uber app, but once outside she spotted a cab parked at a stand down the street. She waved her arm in the air, desperate to get the driver's attention. She saw the turn signal blink on as he signaled his intention to leave the parking spot, breathing a sigh of relief as he waved out the window to indicate he had seen her.

Chris dropped her arm and rubbed her sore belly, taking big breaths of the warm night air. She heard the restaurant door open behind her and turned to see Angel exiting the building.

"Forget about my staff. We can go to my apartment." Angel stepped up to her and put a hand above her elbow to escort her to the car, but Chris didn't move.

"No, I can't, Angel. I have to go home."

Angel turned to face Chris and put her hands on her shoulders, checking her over in the light from a nearby streetlamp. "Are you okay? Did you get hurt in the fall?"

Chris glanced at the cab down the street as he waited for some bicyclers to pass before pulling onto the street. She shrugged Angel's hands off her shoulders. "I'm fine. I just can't go to your apartment."

"Okay, then maybe we can go out tomorrow or next week. There's a place we should get dinner—"

Chris clapped her purse against her forehead. "I can't. We can't go out."

"What?"

Chris raked her fingers through her wavy hair. "You don't understand. There's this...situation..."

Looking at the ground, she rubbed a hand over her face, leaving her palm to cover her mouth as she struggled to figure out what to say.

"Is it your boyfriend? Is it David?"

Chris flopped the hand at her mouth to her side and heaved a big sigh. "I'm sorry, Angel. I had a wonderful evening with you."

Angel nodded. "Let me at least give you a ride home."

The cab was already pulling up to the curb beside them.

"No," said Chris. "I've got to go."

Still refusing to look at Angel, she turned away and took a step toward the car. Then she paused and spoke over her shoulder. "Don't call me."

She climbed into the back seat, and the cab drove away.

CHAPTER NINE

Chris, wearing goggles and a dust mask, switched off her power sander and turned as a car with a burnt-out headlight pulled up to the open garage door of the shop. Mike went out to greet his sister as she got out of the car.

Lucy walked over to him and tossed him a packaged car headlight and her keys. "Thanks, big bro!"

Mike ambled over to the driver's side door to pop the hood while Lucy walked into the building. Chris snapped her power sander back on and the machine whirred to life. She leaned the sander into the wood slab and continued her up and down strokes on the board.

Lucy made herself at home, plopping into a chair at the desk where she snapped open the laptop sitting there and starting to type.

Chris stopped the sander and felt the board. She pulled off the mask and goggles and, setting the power sander down on a nearby table, she grabbed a sanding block. She returned to the board where she felt for a rough spot and started hand sanding.

"Olivia's on State Street," Lucy said as she typed on the laptop.

Chris continued to scrub the sanding block over the board. "What are you doing?"

"I am going to write a terrible review."

"Have you eaten there?"

"Yeah, I love that place! OMG, their beignets are divine. They are going to get the worst review ever!" Lucy started typing. "Is repugnant spelled with an e-n-t or an a-n-t?"

Chris worked a spot on the slab with the sanding block. "You can't do that, Lucy."

Lucy hammered at the keyboard. "Watch me!"

Chris stopped sanding and, walking over to a table with more grits of sandpaper, started poking through them.

"It's a small, local business. You can't leave a fake bad review. I don't want anybody leaving me a fake bad review for this business, so you can't do that to her."

"Ugh!"

"I'm serious. Do not do that on the shop computer. You do not have my permission."

"Fine!" Lucy snapped the laptop shut. "Who is Olivia anyway?"

Chris shrugged and went back to sanding the slab. Lucy turned back to the computer and started typing. "I'll find out," she mumbled. Chris engrossed herself in the slab.

Lucy peered at the screen on the laptop and then dismissed the page and kept typing. "When are you going out with her again?"

"I'm not."

"You said the date went okay."

"I mean, we had an okay time. But she said I wasn't her type. I think she figured out I'm gay."

"I knew it! She only dates straight girls to lure them to the dark side."

Chris scoffed while continuing to make long strokes up and down the board with the sanding block. "Maybe *your* side is the dark side. Maybe the gay side is the light side."

Lucy tapped on the keyboard some more. "You didn't kiss her, did you? I told you she would know you're gay if you kissed her."

"There might have been a kiss."

"I told you she would know!" Lucy stopped typing and began reading the screen intently. "Hey! I found it."

"What?"

"An article about Olivia's when it opened. It's from three years ago." Lucy started reading the article on the screen. "'This Friday a new restaurant opens on State Street called Olivia's Café. Owner Angel Lux is known in the community for her successful food truck, Beignet Done That.' Oh, my god! I remember that truck! That's why Olivia's has such good beignets. After bar time, drunks would literally chase that truck down the street, like little kids after an ice cream truck. If that truck had had a loudspeaker blasting calliope music it would have sucked the patrons out of the bars all over downtown."

"Does it say who Olivia was?"

"Wait a sec. Let me read." Lucy tapped on the touchpad to move the page down. "Says something about Olivia being her partner with the food truck but nothing else. I'll search for something on the truck."

Lucy typed some more and then started to read aloud from another article. "Here's their entry at a food truck fest eight years ago, 'Beignet Done That is operated by the married duo Angel Lux and Olivia Beaumont.'"

"Married?" Chris turned to Lucy and put down the sanding block.

"Yeah. Olivia is Angel's wife. Here's their picture."

Chris walked toward the desk and leaned over Lucy in the chair to look at the webpage over Lucy's shoulder. On the screen was a picture of Angel, around a decade younger, with longer hair and a rounder face. She had an ear-to-ear grin in the picture and her arm was around Olivia, who was also grinning, as they stood in front of their little pink, blue, and white food truck decorated with little French flags.

"Wow." Chris leaned further over Lucy's shoulder to get a better look. "They look so happy. What happened? Are they still married? Are they divorced?"

"Lucky for you I've had a little bit of experience at cyberstalking. We'll type both their names in Google at the same time and we might get something else that links the two." Lucy spoke their names out loud as she typed. "O-li-via Beaumont. An-gel Lux." She hit return.

As Chris and Lucy watched the screen, the first Google hit that came up was a link to an obituary.

"Uh-oh." Lucy clicked the link. Flashing onto the screen was a stunningly beautiful picture of Olivia Beaumont. Lucy began to read the text next to her picture out loud. "'Olivia Beaumont, born in Montreal, Canada, and died in Madison, Wisconsin.'"

"Died?" Chris's hand came up to her mouth in surprise as she sucked in a quick breath.

Lucy continued reading. "'Olivia was a beloved daughter, granddaughter, niece, sister, and spouse. She was a talented cook and excellent baker, and she had a smile that could brighten the world. Leaves behind her business partner and wife of just three years, Angel Lux, her brother...' It goes on."

Chris checked the birth and death dates in the obit.

"That was published five years ago. She was only, like, thirty years old. Does it say how she died?"

"No. It asks for donations to be made to hospice in her name so maybe she was sick?"

Chris stood back up and took a step away from Lucy. "Yeah, maybe so."

"Fine! I won't leave Olivia's a bad review. But only because I don't want to leave this poor woman's namesake a bad review. Angel Lux I don't care about." Lucy thought about that for a moment and then shrugged her shoulders, looking chagrined. "I feel bad her wife died."

Chris leaned back down and looked at the picture of the young, beautiful Olivia Beaumont and wondered what could have killed a person who looked so vibrant and healthy. She wondered, too, why Angel hadn't mentioned the lovely wife who had died so young, even when she had asked about the name attached to the restaurant. Her assumption had been that Angel was a player of some sort, too shallow to ever get involved in a serious relationship. But obviously that was wrong. What else had she misjudged about Angel Lux?

* * *

Angel startled. Something had woken her up. With bleary eyes she checked the time on the clock on the nightstand. One thirty a.m. Despite her fogginess she registered the fact that the numbers on the clock glowed red instead of the warm green she was used to, and she realized she wasn't in her own bed. She felt cool, smooth sheets against her bare skin and memories of less than enthusiastic lovemaking on her partner's behalf a couple of hours earlier seeped into her consciousness. She reached over to feel for the body next to her. But the other side of the bed was cold and empty. The room was dark, but the door was cracked open and a light shone into the room from the hallway. Somewhere past the hallway, she could hear weeping.

Angel fumbled for the light on the nightstand and turned it on. She got up and put on an enormous, oversized robe from the back of a nearby chair—Mike's, she figured—and, holding up the bottom of the robe so she wouldn't trip on it, she padded into the kitchen. There she found Maddie sitting at the kitchen table, wrapped up in a well-fit, fuzzy robe. On the table in front of her was a package labeled 'QuickiePrint!' The big orange cat, Ricky, was dozing in her lap.

Angel took a step closer, and Ricky raised his jowly head at her approach. He flattened his ears, clearly unhappy to see her, and jumped to the floor to amble to another part of the house.

Maddie held her head in one hand and a card from a stack of similar cards in the QuickiePrint box in the other hand while she cried. Angel took another card from the box. Embossed on the front were the names "Mike & Maddie" and a date and inside the card was an unfamiliar name. Table place cards for a wedding, Angel realized. The date printed on the cards was less than two months away.

"Delivered yesterday. It was too late to cancel the order. Thought I'd take a look at them before I threw them away." Maddie sniffled and dragged the sleeve of her robe roughly over her wet face.

Angel put a comforting hand on Maddie's shoulder and sat down next to her. Maddie looked up at her and then reached forward to sadly fondle the fabric of Mike's robe, clearly thinking of him.

Maddie choked as more sobs started to come. "I can't do this anymore."

Angel nodded. She put her hands on Maddie's cheeks, softly wiping the tears away with her thumbs. The pain in her face made tears well up in Angel's eyes. "I know."

They both startled when Maddie's phone rang. Maddie wiped her sleeve again over her dripping face and pulled the phone out of her robe pocket.

Angel wiped a tear out of her own eye. "Who's calling at one thirty in the morning?"

Maddie looked at the phone screen. "It's Lucy. Mike's sister." She stabbed the answer button on the phone. "Lucy, what's wrong?"

* * *

Startled awake by her cell phone, Chris blinked at the clock on her nightstand, trying to read the time. Three forty-seven a.m. Her head cleared. Anticipating an emergency, she grabbed the phone. Lucy's name was displayed on the screen. She hit the answer button. "Hello, Lucy?"

Chris could hear Mike yelling in the background.

"Chris. Can you come to the hospital? Nana is having a heart attack. Mike and Maddie are here. Mike is distraught. He's yelling at the doctors and the security guard. Maddie could always settle him down best, so I called her first—that was probably a mistake—but he won't talk to her. Nana's going into surgery soon to have a clot removed from a coronary artery. But Mike…I'm afraid there's going to be trouble."

"I'll be right there."

Chris whipped on her clothes and ran out the door to her car and sped to the hospital. Texts from Lucy directed her to the correct entrance and the right floor and lobby. In the waiting room she found Lucy and Maddie. Chris hugged them both.

"Where is he right now?"

"He's talking to Nana in her room. I just talked to her. They are getting ready to take her to surgery. At her age it will be pretty risky." Tears began to well in Lucy's eyes. "There's a good chance she won't make it."

"What room?"

"Room 314."

Chris hurried down the hall, checking room numbers. She found the room and rushed inside, stopping herself as soon as she entered. Mike was inside seated in a chair next to the bed. An orderly was at the bed disconnecting cords and wires from the wall, getting ready for the transport to surgery. Mike was crying and holding his grandmother's hand. Her hand was the size of a child's in his large mitt. Chris crept over to stand behind his shoulder.

"Don't worry, Mikey." The old woman's breath was labored, her eyes deeply sunken and her skin an alarming gray color. "If I die, I'll get to be with my Martin again, and that's okay with me."

Mike sniffled. "How long were you married?"

"Fifty-seven years."

Mike smiled. "Wow. Fifty-seven faithful years."

His grandmother laughed and coughed weakly. "Well, they weren't all faithful."

"What? Unfaithful! No, I can't…What?"

"Everybody makes mistakes, sweetie. But you work through the rough patches. It's worth it."

"Time to go, Mrs. Lundgren," said the orderly, unlocking the bed wheels.

Mike stood up and the orderly started pushing the bed toward the hall. Mike held on to his grandmother's hand as long as he could and then let go. As his grandmother was pushed out of the room he turned and with his big hands grabbed Chris, wrapped her up in his big arms, buried his big face in her shoulder, and sobbed.

When he was able to gather his composure, Mike and Chris went out to the hallway to meet with Lucy.

Lucy and Mike hugged, and Chris went to talk to Maddie, who really looked like she needed to say something to Chris. When she got to Maddie and put her hands on her shoulders, the words started to tumble out of Maddie.

"I'm so sorry about the wedding and everything. I know people spent a lot of money—"

"No, no. Don't worry about it."

"I mean, I love him so much! I've just always sort of wondered what it would be like to be with a woman and with the wedding coming up I thought I'd never get another chance—"

"You don't need to expla—"

"I mean, you were always there if I needed to figure this out, but you were Mike's best friend. I couldn't do that to him. Or you—" Maddie choked up and her expression was tortured.

"I understand." Chris took Maddie's hands. "If you ever feel confused, or you just want to ask some questions or talk about anything, I'm here for you."

Maddie nodded. She put a trembling hand to her face, and she looked into Chris's eyes. More tears welled up in Maddie's eyes, and she choked. "Turns out, I'm not gay."

Mike appeared at Chris's shoulder.

Maddie bowed her head and looked away quickly. "Chris, you're here for Mike now. You all don't need me. I'll just go."

She turned to leave, but Mike gently put a hand on her shoulder. Then he turned to Chris. "Chris, okay if Maddie and I talk?"

Chris looked over at Maddie, who nodded, and Chris stepped away. She walked over to Lucy, who was standing at the other end of the hallway. Lucy leaned in to speak quietly to Chris as they watched Mike and Maddie talking down the hall.

"If Nana makes it through surgery, he wants to spend time with her here and at home until she's recovered, but he's worried about the jobs you have booked."

Chris shrugged. "The Sandburg interior job we had booked has fallen way behind. That won't be a problem."

"So you won't have any work then?"

"The market for contractors is pretty tight. I should be able to find some other jobs to do on my own or with a little hired help until he's ready to come back to work."

"Oh, my god. You should have seen him earlier, yelling at the doctors. I thought Security was going to mace him."

"Well, it wouldn't be the first time he's been maced by Security."

"Yeah. He's so damn big and scary when he gets mad if you don't know him."

Suddenly, while Lucy and Chris watched, Mike reached down and embraced Maddie and she reached up to return the hug.

Lucy clapped her hands together. "Well, look at that! Maybe our luck is starting to turn around."

CHAPTER TEN

Chris turned off her car and sat in it a moment, the vehicle quickly heating up in the late afternoon summer sun. She grabbed her laptop on the seat next to her and snapped a large tape measure onto her waistband. She stepped out of the car and locked it up and then walked a couple of blocks to her destination. She looked up at the sign, Olivia's Café. The street was busy with the usual downtown business lunch crowd. Taking a big breath, she stepped through the front door.

At the entrance Chris was greeted by a staff person. She asked if she could talk to the owner for a minute, and then Angel stepped out of the kitchen wearing a white chef's coat trimmed in black and black chef's tie-back skull cap. Upon recognizing Chris, Angel nodded and the two stepped over to a quiet corner of the dining room.

"How is Mike's grandmother doing?"

"Surprisingly well for a seventy-two-year-old woman who just had a blood clot pulled out of an artery in her heart through her leg."

"Oh, that's great!"

"She's in the hospital for a couple more days and then she is going home."

"Wonderful!"

"Mike is going to stay with her for a while."

Angel nodded.

Chris shuffled her feet a little bit, looking at the floor, but then took a big breath and dived in. "I'd like to make a bid on your rooftop deck project if you haven't found a replacement contractor yet."

"Oh." Angel glanced at the laptop Chris was holding. "This is a professional visit."

Chris nodded.

Angel shifted uncomfortably on her feet. "I'm sort of surprised Mike is willing to—"

"He's tied up with his grandmother right now. I'd be working on the project myself, but I could get working on it immediately. Today, even, if we can come to an agreement. I've got some examples on Instagram of the outdoor projects I've done in the past. And I've reviewed your permit and the draft plans and measurements that were approved by city zoning. I've come up with some modifications I think you'd like."

Angel hesitated.

"Could we go up to the rooftop and I'll show you some ideas I have?"

Angel glanced at her uncomfortably and lifted her hand to rub the back of her neck. She started to shake her head.

Chris stepped closer. "Every day the outdoor space is unfinished is another day of revenue lost. I know we don't know each other well, but I think I know you enough that I can say you are a smart businesswoman. The building permit is only good for so long. I've asked around about your previous contractor and he's already moved on to the big rec project by the lake. He's not coming back. I'm guessing you thought you got a really good deal when his bid came in a lot lower than the others?"

Angel stiffened. Her eyes narrowed as she turned a cold glare over Chris's shoulder and into the distance. She guessed some visual was passing through Angel's mind, something like her garroting the contractor's throat. Or possibly garroting his testicles. Most likely, both.

"Well, you can settle that all out in small claims court with him later." Chris heard a low growl emanate from Angel's throat. "Right now, you've got a project on hold while the bank continues to collect on their construction loan, and contractors are busy. I'm sure you've called around and figured that out already. It will be months before anybody else can restart the job, much less get it going today. You'll lose the whole summer."

Angel shook her head and snapped out of her murderous musing. She looked back at Chris and threw up her hands in defeat. "Stop! Stop. You can show me your other projects and your ideas for the space."

Chris grinned.

Angel took off her chef's coat and leaned over to one of her staff. "Send a couple of lemonades to the roof. I'll be up there if you need me."

Chris had been expecting Angel to take her up the stairway from the kitchen again, but this time Angel took her up the second stairway just inside the building entrance, the one that was the stairway intended for customers.

Seeing the rooftop in the sunlight revealed plenty of materials for the construction but no real work done to improve the space except for some beams erected to frame out a structure in the corner and part of the framing for the deck. A spigot had been installed for irrigation and plumbing had been roughed in for a small bar and wait station. A couple of large vents and a large chimney poked out of the roof of the building. There would be no moving those, so Chris would have to work around them, although they did carry over the old industrial feel from the restaurant.

Chris set her laptop down on the decking stacked near the door to the kitchen stairway. Angel looked up at the blue sky and shielded her eyes. "The sun is pretty brutal up here in summer, although the breeze is nice. The plan was to put a pergola over there to provide some shade. They got the beams up for that, but that's about it except for the deck framing over there."

Someone brought up lemonades from the kitchen and set them down next to Chris's laptop and then left. Angel took one for herself and handed the other to Chris, who set it down before starting to poke through the building materials on the roof. Decking boards, aluminum framing pieces, partial trim work. No hardware. "Is all of the decking and framing here?"

"I believe so."

Chris nodded. "That makes things a lot easier." She bent down low to check the slope of the roof. She pointed at a part of the half-constructed aluminum deck framing. "You'll have a problem with drainage over there. I'll need to redo some of that framing to get it oriented to drain properly, but fortunately they didn't get too far on framing. The beams for the pergola look well installed so those should work fine."

Angel took a big swig of lemonade and put the glass down. "Show me your portfolio."

Chris came over to the laptop and snapped it open. The laptop blinked to life and connected to the hotspot on Chris's phone. She navigated to her portfolio, and they went through the images. She started to talk about the project plans that had been uploaded to the city planning website, but Angel put up a hand.

"Give me an estimate. Time and cost."

Chris ended her presentation with an estimate that acknowledged her position as someone operating with a not-yet-established reputation. She knew Angel couldn't turn it down. Two hours later they clinked their lemonades on the deal.

"You're right about the bank loan. I can carry the payments on the construction loan for a while but not for months. I need this space generating revenue yesterday. I don't want it done just as the snow starts to fly."

"I'll go back to the shop where I can print up the contract so we can get it signed," Chris said, smiling.

"Would you like to do that here? I can get you connected to the printer in the office. Then you can get started right away."

"Sure!"

Angel grabbed their glasses and dropped them at the dishwashing station before leading her past the pantry to the office.

Chris noticed the desk, which was now just a plywood board on top of some stacked milk crates. She felt a hot blush rise up her throat to her cheeks and noticed Angel glancing at her burning face and grinning slightly.

Angel quickly pulled forward the desk chair and sat down while Chris put her laptop on the makeshift desk. "Yeah, I haven't had time to replace the desk yet."

Angel snapped the laptop open, and Chris leaned over Angel to tap in a password to unlock it. For a moment, Chris let herself appreciate Angel's closeness, before she corrected herself and took a step back.

She rubbed a palm over her face, willing the last of the blush to dissipate. "I know we have a…um…short history, but I'd like to keep this professional."

"Of course." Angel first navigated to the Wi-Fi setting to connect to the restaurant network and then navigated to the printer settings and made some additional adjustments. The printer on the file cabinet blinked to life. Angel got out of the chair and let Chris sit down. "I'll leave you to it. I'll be on the cook line when you are ready for a signature."

The bustle in the kitchen increased as the dinner crowd began to arrive. Chris got to work on the contract and a spreadsheet with her estimates. An hour later, as the kitchen started to buzz like an angry beehive, she printed out the contract and waved Angel over from the cook line. After a quick review of the details and the cost-out, she nodded. Chris handed her a pen and she signed it.

"I'm not sure how good you are at patio construction, but you are a damn fine saleswoman."

Chris grinned. Angel returned the grin with a half-smile that crinkled the corners of her eyes.

"I can scan the signed contract on the printer, and then I will cut you a payment for half so you can get started right away. Sound good?"

Chris nodded. Angel held up the pen for Chris. She wrapped her hand around it, but Angel didn't let go, and they stood there for a moment with their hands together around the pen.

Angel let go of the pen. "I hope David appreciates what a lucky man he is."

Chris looked down at her shoes, tucking the pen in a breast pocket. "I'll be here first thing in the morning."

* * *

"Chris! Good news!" Mike's voice sounded joyful over the phone. "We're taking Nana home from the hospital today. In fact, we're getting her in the car now."

Chris heard Lucy's voice in the background as she directed her grandmother into the car.

"That's great, Mike!"

"The doctor said she's doing really well. I'm going to stay home with her for a couple weeks, but by then she should be okay on her own. Have you got work to do for a while?"

"Yeah. I booked a job that will keep me busy." Chris juggled her phone while she steered one-handed into a parking lot and pulled her car into a spot in front of a building with a sign that read, Linda Pawlowski, CPA.

"Have you been to the accountant's yet?"

"I'm pulling in there right now." Chris threw the car into park and turned off the engine. She glanced nervously at the front door. "Are you sure we want to go with Linda?"

"I've heard she's a really good CPA. And she charges a reasonable rate. Plus, she gave us business, so we give her business. That's how it works."

Chris fumbled with the piles of financial paperwork on her passenger seat. "I'm sort of scared to go in there."

"Linda won't bother you. You made it pretty clear you weren't interested when you threw that glass across her kitchen and ran out the door. Besides, I like her. I might even invite her to the wedding if it's ever back on."

"I didn't throw the—"

Chris paused as she heard Mike say, "Maddie, I'll get in the back with Gram."

"Back on? Wait. Is Maddie with you right now?"

"Yeah. Maddie and Lucy are both here with me at the hospital." Chris heard the grin in Mike's voice.

"Are you and Maddie…working things out?"

Mike paused. "I think so. I think maybe we can work it out."

* * *

The next morning Chris arrived at Olivia's at the same time as the breakfast crew. Loading and unloading vehicles were allowed on State Street, so with a little help from Jasper she got a table saw and two chop saws up to the worksite, one for the wood boards and the second for the aluminum joists. She brought up the rest of the tools and the hardware she would need by herself and parked the work truck in a nearby ramp.

On the roof she set up a staging area, placing a temporary plywood floor over the rubber roof membrane. There she could cut and rip boards safely on the only part of the rooftop with a little shade from a next-door building. She would have to carry each board across the roof from the pile by the door, but it was worth it to be out of the sun for at least a while. She set up the second saw by the aluminum joists. The racket from that thing would be impressive.

Once the deck was installed, she'd use her cabinetry skills to install the wait station and small bar, to be placed next to the kitchen stairway on the west wall.

She'd also have to pick up a few more materials for planters that had been added to the plan to conceal some plumbing vent stacks and one large air handling vent. Fortunately, most of the mechanicals were on the northeast corner of the roof, where they were already concealed behind a six-foot cedar fence. A second air handling vent, however, was unfortunately placed near the east-west centerline of the roof and closer to the lake side of the building. Moving it was impossible given the budget. Attempting to conceal it would have been awkward due to the prominent location. In the end, it didn't pose a safety hazard, so leaving it and using the large, industrial-looking sheet metal object to repeat the factory chic of the dining room seemed like the best way to handle the problem.

She would need another couple of days to build and stain the pergola in the southwest corner; it would keep the direct summer sun off at least some of the lunch- and dinner-time diners on the patio. Tables not under the pergola would require shade umbrellas.

The pergola would also be used as a base for the lighting that would need to be installed to brighten evenings on the patio. She could hang all the lighting and cable it up as appropriate but, per zoning codes, a licensed electrician would need to do the final connections. And, of course, the city would not allow any public occupancy until an inspector came out to look at the work. After that, getting the tables and chairs delivered and set up would be a breeze.

It certainly wasn't a big space, by any means. But Olivia's wasn't a big restaurant and already had long lines in summer waiting for a table. With the rooftop deck Olivia's would have about sixteen more tables and seating for maybe fifty more people, which would add significantly to the business's bottom line. But the patio was big enough and would be a lot of work for Chris, given the lack of help.

Chris planned on eight- to ten-hour days and maybe working through the weekend if needed, depending on the weather. If all the stars aligned, she'd have it done in two weeks and finish on a Friday. She'd get a nice, fat check from Angel, and then she and Mike could return to their regular business, and she wouldn't have to see Angel again, with her beautiful blue eyes, strong jaw, high cheekbones, and stunning figure.

Chris spent the rest of the day lugging up materials from the shop truck and running around town getting the supplies she needed, moving boards around the rooftop, and setting up the equipment. Looking around, she realized with a good deal of satisfaction that in the morning she'd be able to start the actual partial demo and construction. She pulled a handkerchief out of her pocket and mopped some of the sweat off her face and hands, a good layer of grime coming off with the sweat.

"Chair?"

Chris turned to see Angel holding out a chair while Jo carried a small table and set it down next to Angel.

"Bring another chair, please." Jo nodded and headed for the stairway.

Jasper arrived on the rooftop carrying a tray with a large glass of ice water and a dinner plate which he set on the table.

Angel waved Chris over and patted the chair. "Come. I want you to try out a new recipe for me."

"Me?" Chris walked over to the table. "I'm no culinary expert."

"Neither are ninety-nine-point-nine percent of my customers."

Chris sat in the chair. Angel put a napkin on her lap. Chris lunged for the water and started to chug it.

"Bring more water," Angel told Jasper. He headed for the kitchen stairway. Jo showed up with the extra chair and set it at the table across from Chris where Angel sat down. Angel reached forward to turn the pastry-laden plate to just the right angle in front of Chris. "There has been a bumper crop of tomatoes this summer and I can get them dirt cheap at the farmers market on Saturdays. This is called a tomato tart."

Chris set down the half-empty water glass and looked at the plate. "Looks sort of like a pizza."

"Similar. But the tomato is forward, not the cheese. It's a recipe from the Provence region in France. The crust is a crunchy puff pastry. You'll taste Dijon mustard and cracked pepper. A good dollop of olive oil over the tomatoes and breadcrumbs to top it off before it goes in the oven. Very simple. Do you like tomatoes?"

Chris nodded. She awkwardly started to stab at the tart with her knife and fork.

"Pick it up and eat it. Like a pizza. Like this." Angel grabbed the tart off the plate and held it out for Chris. She took a bite.

Her eyes went wide. "Yum!" She took the tart from Angel and took a big bite. "Gosh, that's so good!" she mumbled through a mouth full of tomato tart.

"It's the heirloom tomatoes. They have a lot more flavor than what you are used to from the average grocery store."

"That's a win if you are going to sell them at the restaurant," Chris said between another couple of big bites of tart.

Angel laughed as Jasper arrived and put a pitcher of ice water on the table before leaving again. "Great, I'll do that. You sure look like you are enjoying it. I should have brought one for myself."

Chris looked at the single tart she was holding in her hands as Angel filled her glass with more ice water. "Would you like to join me?"

"No, I...ah..."

"Angel? There you are!"

Chris and Angel turned to see a young woman adorned in a black miniskirt, a tight neon pink tank top, and a spangled purse step onto the roof from the kitchen stairway. She headed over to the table and Chris watched in alarm as the heels of her stilettos sank into the rubber membrane of the roof, leaving deep impressions in the surface.

"God, it's hot up here! Babe, I thought we were going out for drinks and dinner. How about TGI Friday's? They have the best margaritas."

Chris jumped to her feet and made a "stop" hand at the young woman before she took another step. Startled, she stopped walking. Chris turned to Angel. "The shoes."

Angel looked at the young woman's shoes. Realization crossing her face, she jumped up and ran to the woman, taking her by the arm and escorting her back to the stairwell. "Wait for me in the dining room. I'll be right down."

"What? What's the problem? Who's that woman? Why is she so sweaty? And why are there all these boards around?"

Angel led her into the stairway and closed the door. Then she walked back to the table and sat down.

Chris took another drink of water.

"She's pretty. Is she your date tonight?" Chris asked, noticing Angel's light linen slacks and periwinkle blouse buttoned low to display her cleavage, the light touch of lipstick, and the eyeliner that accentuated her eyes, a bright sapphire blue in the sunlight of the rooftop, making them even more captivating.

"Yeah. We'll see how it goes. We're not really clicking, so this might be one of those first date, last date kind of evenings."

Chris nodded, taking a small bite of the tart.

"What time will you be coming in, in the mornings?" Angel asked.

"Early. I'd rather not be out here at the hottest part of the day, so I plan on getting here as soon as your breakfast crew gets in."

"They are here by six a.m."

"Great. I'll be here then. The upper floors of a lot of the businesses here on State Street are residential apartments so I won't be able to operate all of the equipment until a little later in the morning, but I still should be able to keep myself busy with tasks that aren't too noisy until then."

"Neighbors don't like power saws and air compressors at six o'clock in the morning?"

Chris smiled. "They hate it! They hate it anyway, but especially at six o'clock in the morning. Then I'll probably knock off a couple of hours in the middle of the day when the sun is at its worst, but I'll be back later and finish the day around four thirty."

Chris ate the last bit of her tomato tart and took another big drink of water. Angel's phone dinged in her pocket, indicating that she had received a text message. She ignored it.

"Great. Usually, we've got a lull around four before the dinner rush starts. Maybe you'd like to be our tester for the evening specials. You can let us know what you think before we make the final decision on the pricing."

Angel's phone dinged again.

Chris nodded. "Sure."

Angel smiled. Her phone dinged a third time.

Chris set the water glass down. "That's probably your date."

Angel sighed, pulled the phone out of her pocket, and glanced at the screen. "Yeah, she's ready for those margaritas."

"Hope it goes well tonight," Chris said, wiping her fingers on her napkin and thinking, *I hope it goes really badly tonight!* "Thank you for the tart."

Angel nodded. She stood up and smiled. "Leave the dishes. The staff will take care of it. See you tomorrow."

Chris watched Angel's hips sway lightly as she walked across the roof before departing through the kitchen stairway.

* * *

Fortunately, no more of Angel's dates showed up on the roof after that first one.

Chris had worked out a schedule that avoided the restaurant's busiest times so she wouldn't disturb the diners with any construction racket. Getting in early, she'd stain boards first thing and then start arranging them on the aluminum joists. The previous contractor's plans had described a floating roof system so there was no need to pierce the rubber membrane to make any attachments. At nine a.m. she'd get started with the air compressor, screw guns, and power saws that could cut through solid boards and beams of aluminum like butter.

Then at ten a.m., after torturing her all morning with the smells of bacon and sausage sizzling on a grill and fresh pastries being baked, the kitchen staff would arrive at the table and chairs Angel had left on the roof and set a picnic of what she was assured was an authentic French breakfast, with fresh ground coffee and just squeezed orange juice, various fruits, and flaky croissants or fresh from the oven brioche.

The heavy bacon and eggs, sausage, potatoes, hams, hashes, and cheese omelets washed down with bloody marys and mimosas were all for the downtown workers who demanded it. Angel's staff served Chris different little jams for her bread, including a mouthwatering bitter orange jam, a bright rhubarb preserve, and a heavenly blackberry spread. She got salted butter for her bread or a sweet butter. She was served yogurts and nuts and, on occasion, a little pastry called a *pain au chocolat*, which was like a croissant with chocolate bits. Chris loved them fresh out of the oven. And, of course, beignets! Endless piles of them! Little, fluffy, heavenly clouds dusted with powdered sugar. They weren't allowed to sit around and any that were older than a few hours were left in a basket next to the door between the kitchen and the dining room and snatched up and eaten by the staff. Chris poked her head in the kitchen throughout the day to check for more of them.

At eleven a.m. she knocked off to avoid the worst of the midday heat and head home to do some chores or errands or just take a nap. At two p.m. she would return and work till around four thirty when Angel would come out with a picnic dinner, and they would discuss the progress on the patio and finalize design decisions and plans for the perennials and other plantings. At Angel's request, Chris was going to add a vertical garden on the south-facing wall where Angel could grow fresh herbs. It had been dutifully added as an amendment to the contract, although that still needed to be signed.

Chris loved these early evening meals with Angel, brief though they were so Angel could get to the line for the dinner rush. As four thirty approached she found herself constantly glancing at the stairway door, waiting for her to appear. Her stomach got used to the schedule after only a few days and would growl starting around four; Olivia's really had some amazing chefs. Chris's heart growled for Angel. She was such enjoyable company, with her witty sense of humor and her warm, thoughtful interest in what Chris had to say.

During a dinner on a particularly hot day, as Angel repeatedly filled her water glass, never letting it get below half full, Chris had opened up about her parents' divorce when she was five and the string of boyfriends her mom had allowed to live with them after that. Some of the men Chris never took a shine to and she was happy to see them go. Her mom liked nice guys, though, and most of them had been really nice guys. They would take Chris out in the yard and throw a ball with her or come to her games to watch her play soccer or show her how to fix cars and build bird houses. She loved all of that.

They always left eventually. Her mom was never one to be "tied down." Soon Chris had learned it was just better not to get attached. It had all worked out fine in the end.

It wasn't a story she told a lot of people, but Angel had listened attentively and had followed up with a gentle sort of questioning that had caused Chris to completely open up with her. Only a handful of people knew her story. That included Mike and him only because she had grown up next door to him and he had seen the play-by-play of her entire childhood.

Mike had always been like a big brother to her, although they were the same age. Lucy was a couple of years younger than they were, so Chris had always been closer to Mike than Lucy. Then there was the fact that Chris had always been a tomboy and wanted to play with trucks instead of dolls and play sports with the boys instead of playing house with the girls. That meant that she and Mike had more in common anyway.

Chris had been heartbroken when she had introduced him to a girl who had answered an ad she had posted for a roommate and the girl and Mike had instantly hit it off. And now they were getting married. Or *maybe* they were getting married. Or, more likely, maybe they weren't getting married at all at this point.

As Chris and Angel had dinner that afternoon, Angel wrapped some ice cubes in a napkin and laid it across the back of Chris's neck to cool her off. Chris, the welcome cold from the water dripping down her collar, tried to reconcile this person with the relationship-wrecking, predatory stalker at bars looking for intoxicated, confused women to seduce and destroy that she knew Angel to be, but every day making that connection got just a little fuzzier for Chris.

By the end of the first week of work Chris realized she physically ached when she saw Angel. She was no longer sure if the pain was due to the intense physical labor she was performing or if it was a deeper ache, desire that was becoming painful to keep pushed down. Being honest with herself, she knew it was probably both.

* * *

Angel leaned over the table of produce and keenly eyed the tomatoes. She picked one up and gave it a gentle squeeze and then sniffed the blossom end. It smelled like summer. They weren't the prettiest, but that wouldn't matter once they were sliced and cooked into a tart.

Angel nodded at the woman manning the stand. Behind her Jasper started packing several pounds of the tomatoes into the wagon the restaurant used for these trips to the Saturday morning Dane County farmers market, the largest producers-only farmers market in the country.

She went to examine the rhubarb, wondering if Chris would like a rhubarb pie. Angel thought she might like it extra tart, but she'd add a dollop of whipped cream to the plate, just in case. She imagined Chris enthusiastically digging into the pie and smiling up at her as the tart rhubarb mixed with the sweet whipped cream on her palate.

"Angel? Why are you smiling? Did you hear a word I said?"

Angel wiped the smile off her face and picked up a ruby red rhubarb stalk and examined the cut end to judge the freshness of the cut. "Yeah. Something about…something."

"You seem sort of distracted lately."

"I do? Hmm."

They moved on to the next stall where Angel stopped, the rhubarb there catching her eye. She grabbed a stalk and sniffed the end. It smelled bright and clean and tart. Pink, clear juice beaded up at the cut, indicating a cut probably only a few hours old. She signaled to Jasper, who started putting rhubarb in a bag.

Yes, the remodel was a distraction, but necessary. The kitchen could service more tables but expanding the old building in any direction was not an option. Adding tables to the rooftop was.

The fiasco with the first contractor had been a blow, but Chris had been an excellent choice as a replacement. The construction was coming along smoothly, despite the fact that it was a one-person operation. Chris was confident in her work and really seemed to enjoy what she was doing.

When she got a chance, Angel would watch Chris at work. Lifting and carrying things with those strong, tanned arms. Competently cutting boards and drilling holes with those solid, sure hands. And that ass! Wow, that beautiful bottom! Curves for days that she just couldn't get out of her mind. Too bad Chris had taken herself out of the dating pool.

God damned David!

Yeah. She was distracted. She wondered for a moment if she was distracted by work or by Chris. She admitted to herself that, if she was being honest, it was probably both.

CHAPTER ELEVEN

Angel carefully sliced a piece of beautiful rhubarb pie with a perfect golden-brown crust and set it on a plate next to a snow-white dollop of whipped cream. She put another slice on a plate for herself and then fixed up the rest of the dinner plates. She had just sent Jo up to the roof with a pitcher of ice water and the table setting to put together on the little table and chairs set up on the roof for these dinners. Jo's arrival on the roof would be Chris's cue to head to the restroom to quickly wash her face and arms and get some of the day's grit and grime off her skin.

Today's table talk would probably be about bolts and lug nuts and proper torque as these seemed to be important details for the pergola going up soon. Angel would have absolutely nothing to add to the conversation, but she would listen in fascination, if only because Chris's intense interest in the topic was so infectious. Even a primer on the RPMs of a table saw could hold Angel's interest if Chris were the one doing the talking, her hazel eyes glinting with enthusiasm and white teeth flashing behind her bare, pink lips.

As she arranged the plates on the tray, Angel wondered if this was what Chris and David discussed at the dinner table—RPMs and torque pressures—when he was home from building electrical substations around the country. Maybe that's why she loved him?

Angel was quite certain that Chris was not one hundred percent straight and probably not even fifty percent straight. Maybe not even as much as twenty-five percent straight. Not after the way she had kissed Angel and wrapped her legs around her in the office. Not after the shy glances she saw Chris give her in the kitchen when she would come inside for a glass of water or a beignet. At their dinners too, she noticed, Chris's hazel eyes seemed irresistibly drawn to her mouth and her throat and, when her chef's coat was undone, down to the spot near the top open button of her shirt.

Angel reached up and undid the top buttons on her chef's coat, picked up the tray, and headed for the roof. There she found Jo standing at the table, now set with napkins and silverware and the large pitcher of ice water and glasses, and completely absorbed by a sight on the roof. She looked up to see what Jo was watching and saw Chris, standing next to a ladder, one end of a pergola beam in an overhead bracket and the other balanced on her strong, broad shoulder.

With slow, careful steps Chris climbed up the ladder. Below the tight cargo shorts she was wearing bulged the muscles in her calves and thighs, accentuated by the extra weight of the beam. Once she was high enough, she settled herself into the ladder, deftly lifted the beam off her shoulder, and placed it in its slot over the rafter of the pergola. Her tanned arms gleamed with sweat and honey-blond hairs that had escaped from her ponytail fringed her face.

It was then that Angel realized Chris's generous bottom, gifted to her by some gracious goddess, wasn't just a place to store calories but also the product of the hard, physical labor associated with bending, lifting, and carrying for hours every day. It would be a crime not to admire that ass, Angel thought to herself. Apparently, Jo had the exact same thought.

She set the tray down on the table, startling Jo, who sheepishly dropped her gaze from Chris's backside to the floor. Angel nodded toward the stairway in a get-back-to-work manner, and Jo hurriedly departed. Her exit caught Chris's attention, and she looked over her shoulder to see Angel putting dinner on the table. Chris grinned and Angel smiled back.

"Just have to finish one thing up here."

Angel arranged the plates on the table, thinking David was a lucky man. Even if Chris wasn't a hundred percent straight, she must have had at least some attraction to David. Clearly, she had committed to him even if they weren't talking about a specific marriage date yet. Angel recalled what it felt like to be deeply committed to her own wife before she died.

Angel filled the water glasses and sighed at being reminded of what that commitment felt like after what happened with Maddie. As condensation dripped down the sides of the water pitcher like tears, she recalled the tears of deep pain and regret she had seen in Maddie's eyes when Maddie had betrayed her commitment to Mike.

In the past Angel had always felt no responsibility for the decisions of another grown woman to sleep with her. Any woman was free to do what she wanted with her body and with whomever she wanted. She still believed that. But the collapse of Maddie's relationship wouldn't have happened but for her deciding to pursue Maddie at the club despite the engagement ring on her finger. She had assumed that any unavailable woman who made herself available for a secret tryst probably wasn't in a great relationship anyway, and if the relationship ended as a result of their indiscretions it was likely for the better. But that didn't seem to be the case with Maddie. With Maddie, it seemed like her decision to cheat had been a mistake. A mistake Angel had been all too happy to lead her to.

It made her so angry that the universe allowed unhappy people to continue in unhappy relationships while her joyful marriage had been promptly snuffed out with Olivia's death. But the brutal end to her marriage hadn't been Mike and Maddie's fault. Nor was it the fault of all the other couples she had interfered with. Yet she had made them all pay for it. Angel recognized a heavy feeling in her chest. That feeling, she realized, was guilt. And she didn't like it.

Angel looked up to see if Chris was almost done—just in time to see Chris rushing to back down the ladder.

"I should wash up—" She missed the last step and stumbled backward, catching herself with her hand on a nearby worktable. Several woodworking tools were knocked onto the floor, including a sharp-looking chisel.

"You okay?" Angel called to Chris, who was holding her left hand.

Chris nodded and walked over, laughing at herself. "Yeah. I was in too much of a rush to get to dinner."

Angel glanced at her left hand, which she was holding close to her chest with her right. A growing bloom of bright red blood the color of the rhubarb filling on the plate was spreading across the front of her shirt from under her hand.

"I might need a Band-Aid."

"Shit." Angel quickly strode over and reached for her hand. "Let me see." Angel examined the two-inch cut along the heel of her palm. It was bleeding profusely, the deepness of the cut obscured by the blood. Grabbing the dish towel on her shoulder, Angel deftly wrapped it around Chris's wrist and hand. "Come on. We'll clean that up in the kitchen and get a better look."

Chris pointed at the table with her uninjured hand. "But dinner—"

"This first."

Taking the hand that was still pointing at the table, she led her down the stairs and to a big sink in the kitchen. She got the water running while Chris unwrapped the dish towel. Angel took the hand, which was still bleeding quite a bit, and shoved it under the water, making sure to get the cut directly under the spray. Chris didn't even flinch. She dispensed some soap into her hand and removed Chris's hand from the water just long enough to carefully lather it up. Then she put it back under the cold water. "Let that run for a while."

After a few minutes she shut off the water and wrapped a clean towel around Chris's hand. "Let's sit down in the office."

She led her to the office, where she sat Chris down in the desk chair, her hand up on the makeshift plywood desk. She returned to the kitchen to grab a first aid kit and another chair, brought them back into the office, and sat down at the desk next to Chris. She pumped some hand sanitizer from a bottle on the desk onto her hands and rubbed it in vigorously.

"Okay, let's take a look." Angel carefully unwrapped the dish towel, taking note of the volume of blood that had seeped through to stain the snow-white fabric. Any more blood than that and she would have wrapped another towel around it and taken Chris straight to urgent care, but it didn't seem too bad, so she continued to unwrap.

"Sorry about the towel. I—"

"Don't worry about it." Angel cleared the last bit of the towel from Chris's hand. Holding the hand in her own, she turned it to get a good view of the cut in the light. She tugged at the edges gently to gauge the depth of the injury.

"Can you do this?" Angel held up her own hand, palm up, and slowly flexed each finger down individually toward the palm, starting with the little finger and moving toward the thumb.

Chris repeated the action on her injured hand. "Yeah. I can do that."

"Good." Angel glanced up at Chris and noticed that despite her cool as a cucumber exterior, a paleness was starting to settle into her cheeks.

Angel reached up to put a comforting hand on her shoulder. "I think the bleeding has pretty much stopped. It's deep, though. If we go into urgent care, they might want to put a couple of stitches in that. How's your health insurance?"

Chris winced for the first time. "You mean my high-deductible, catastrophic-only health insurance?"

Angel nodded and then grabbed some bandaging material from the first aid kit. She held it up. "Are you up for an amateur repair job then? I work in a professional kitchen, so I have a lot of experience bandaging up cuts."

"Yeah, let's do it."

Angel got to work, carefully smearing some antibiotic ointment around the cut and then folding some gauze down to size to lay over the injury. Then she started applying the self-adhesive bandage, wrapping it a couple of times around Chris's wrist and then around the palm, over the thumb to the back of the hand. Her palm was calloused from the hard, physical labor she did every day, the nails were short and clean, and the long fingers looked strong. It was a very capable hand. She pictured it moving up her body—from her thigh to her hip to her waist—and imagined what that strong, capable hand could do to her. How Chris could use those long fingers to drive her completely wild.

She physically shook her head, trying to rattle those thoughts out of her brain, making like she was adjusting herself in the chair to cover the action, and then returned to her task. She wrapped the bandage a couple more times around the palm before finishing the last wrap around the wrist and snipping the bandage tape from the roll.

She set the scissors and tape on the table. "There. Not a bad job if I do say so myself."

Chris picked up her hand to examine the bandage. "Nice work, Dr. Lux. If I ever need an emergency appendectomy and don't have the cash to cover a co-pay, I'll know where to come."

"Cuts and minor burns I treat for free, but a kitchen table appendectomy might cost you."

Chris laughed. Angel noted her good humor despite the injury to her hand, which probably hurt like a son-of-a-bitch. "Burns are free, too? Gosh, I could have used you when I got this from a heat gun." She pointed at a patch of white skin on her tanned left forearm. "I didn't know what to do about that when it happened."

"Keep a burn clean so it doesn't get infected and take lots of ibuprofen. That's my experience with burns." Angel pushed up the sleeves on her jacket to show off scars on her arms and hands she had acquired from oven burns over the years. Chris pointed to a particularly impressive purple scar that covered a solid inch on Angel's wrist. "From a stock pot, about a year ago."

"Good one. Check this out." Chris showed her a three-inch scar on her forearm near her elbow, little white dots next to the line of the scar clearly demarcating where the stitches had been. "Hit a knot in a piece of wood. The table saw kicked it back and drove it two inches into my arm."

"How many stitches?"

"Five."

"I got that beat." Angel showed her a half-circle scar on her right thumb. "Mandolin slicer injury. Almost took the pad clean off. They sewed it back on. Twelve stitches."

Chris shuddered. "Yeah, you win. That's bad. Though I'm kinda glad to be the loser in this game."

Angel laughed. Then she saw Chris's eyes dart to the scar through her right eyebrow and then politely back down to the bandage on her hand as she fiddled with the edge of the tape. Angel touched the scar.

"How did that happen?" Chris asked shyly.

"Oh, that didn't happen in the kitchen." She licked the thumb with the mandolin scar and smoothed down the wild tuft on her brow. "That happened before I started cooking. When I was young." Angel started to pack the bandaging equipment back in the first aid kit. "And very stupid." She glanced up at Chris. "But the girl was very pretty." She rearranged some of the items in the kit to make them fit better. "Let's just say I wasn't nearly as good of a skateboarder as I thought I was."

"Oooh." Chris nodded her head in understanding. "Well, I hope your pretty girl was very impressed."

"I think the volume of blood impressed her a lot." Angel snapped the kit shut. "I certainly made an impression on that metal handrail with my head."

They both laughed and she and Chris stood up from the table.

"I hope at least you got a date with her after that."

Angel grinned. "In fact, I married her."

Chris took in a sharp breath.

Angel pointed at her bare left ring finger. "Not married anymore," she said reassuringly.

Chris started to fidget, making more noticeable the bloodstain on the front of her shirt. It looked like someone had dumped a glass of red wine down it. "Speaking of blood, let me get you a fresh T-shirt. I know I have one in here."

She pulled open the bottom file cabinet drawer and rummaged through the supplies there, which included a few spare clothes in case a big kitchen mess got past her chef's coat. She pulled out an old but clean T-shirt and put it on the desk in front of Chris.

"Thanks!"

Angel backed away as Chris started to pull off her shirt, which got stuck over her head when she couldn't grasp it with her injured left hand as she had intended.

"Here, let me help." Angel stepped up and grabbed the part of the shirt stuck on her left arm and carefully guided her injured hand out through the arm hole. Chris pulled the rest of the soiled shirt off over her head, and Angel suddenly found herself standing so close to Chris, clad in just her bra, that she could feel the heat radiating off her skin. Chris blushed.

Angel cleared her throat and stepped back while Chris quickly grabbed the other shirt. Fumbling to get it over her head, she was again defeated by her injured hand. Angel stepped in again.

"Just a little platonic help." Angel gave Chris a shaky smile and reached up to get the shirt over her head and past the ponytail which was becoming quickly undone in the struggle with the shirt. Together they got the shirt on, and Angel grabbed the hem to pull the bottom of the shirt down. She smoothed the fabric over Chris's sides and felt Chris tremble under her hands.

Chris stepped back and yanked off the ponytail holder, moving to put the ponytail back in, but, assembling a ponytail being another two-handed job, she immediately gave up. She tucked the band in her shorts pocket and flipped her blond hair, which fell in messy waves over her shoulders. Angel imagined

Chris waking up in the morning, her hair in honey-blond waves over the pillow, well mussed after an active night of sex.

Angel shook her head again. Why the hell couldn't she keep thoughts of sex out of her brain when she was around Chris? She looked warily at the other woman, rattled by the unreasonable idea that Chris might be reading her mind. Instead, she was just looking at her with large, sad eyes.

"Dinner?"

Angel smiled. "I'll have Jo bring a couple fresh plates to the roof for us. Along with some ibuprofen."

Chris grinned.

Chris loved the pie. They ate it first, devouring it, with the injury to her hand not affecting her appetite in the least. The dinner plate held a chicken breast in a thick, buttery, lemon sauce. Angel insisted on cutting the meat for Chris so she didn't have to struggle with her bandaged hand. Chris resisted only slightly before giving in to the demand.

Chris talked about bolts, lug nuts, and torque, as Angel had expected. As she busily sopped up some sauce with a piece of chicken on her fork, Angel took a big drink of ice water and asked, "So when is David coming back?"

"David?"

"Yeah. David." Angel's eyebrows squeezed together in confusion as Chris enthusiastically put the fork in her mouth and returned to the last piece of chicken on her plate. Did she remember the name wrong?

"Your boyfriend?"

Chris's fork froze. She glanced up at Angel and then started moving the chicken slowly around the plate again, picking up every bit of sauce. "David is away. I…he…not sure." She gave a large shrug. "They ran into some issues and the job is delayed. Might be days before they are back on track. Weeks even. More water?" Chris held out her glass. Angel dutifully filled it.

"Oh, that's too bad. That must be hard on you."

Chris took a big drink of the ice water, nodding at Angel's remark at the same time. "Not so bad," she said into the glass.

"Really? Because I imagine it must be hard—"

Chris hopped to her feet, wiping her mouth with her napkin and tossing it on the empty plate. "Say, I have in my car the amendment to our contract to install the vertical gardens. Would you mind signing that?"

Angel nodded, folded her napkin on the table, and stood up. "I'll follow you out."

Once at her Subaru, Chris took the contract amendment out of her briefcase, talking about the changes she had made, the fees they had discussed, and the materials she had planned to use for the installation.

Angel eyed the beat-up Subaru with random tools in the back. She looked back at Chris, unable to keep the suspicion out of her gaze.

* * *

Chris, Mike, and Grandma Lundgren sat at the loaded picnic table on Lucy's deck. Lucy stood at the grill, flipping burgers. "Why am I doing this? Grilling isn't my job."

Chris held up her hand, now dressed with only a large, beige Band-Aid patch across the palm. "Injured."

Mike popped open a soda can and poured the drink into a glass of ice for his grandmother. "You should try some liquid bandage on that. Works pretty good."

"Yeah. I'm going to put some on tonight."

"Did that happen on the job? How's that coming?"

"Should be done tomorrow, right on schedule."

"Who's it for again?" asked Mike.

"A small restaurant downtown," said Chris, piling chips on her plate. "You wouldn't have heard of it. Hey, did you guys read about those wildfires?"

"I'd love to see what you built without me," continued Mike. "What's the name of the restaurant?"

Chris put her glass of lemonade up to her mouth and mumbled into it. "Olivia's."

Mike cupped his hand around his ear. "What?"

Lucy swished onto the patio holding up the platter of meat. "I come bearing burgers!"

Maddie followed Lucy, saying with equal enthusiasm, "And I have plates and buns!"

Maddie set her load on the table and turned to Mike's grandma. "Can I fix you up a plate, Mrs. Lundgren?"

The old lady nodded.

Chris noticed that before grabbing a plate Maddie reached for Mike's hand and gave it a little squeeze. The two smiled at each other before Maddie turned back to Mrs. Lundgren. "Mustard or ketchup?"

Lucy took a big bite of her burger and Maddie took a swig from her iced tea. The laughter and shrieks of children playing in a nearby yard tumbled past the deck on the summer breeze. A lawn mower hummed away in the distance.

Maddie turned to Lucy. "I heard you've been dating someone new."

Lucy waggled her eyebrows up and down and then grinned at Maddie. "I'm always dating someone new."

They both giggled.

Mike turned to Chris. "What did you say was the name of the place where you've been working? Olivia's?"

Maddie sprayed iced tea across the table, and Lucy choked on her burger. Chris froze.

Mike leaned over to wipe iced tea off the table and looked quizzically at the women. "What?"

Lucy paused for a moment and then put her hand gently on Mike's. "Mike—"

Chris leapt up from the table and ran to Lucy, dragging her out of the chair. "Lucy, I think something is burning in the kitchen!"

Lucy threw her hands in the air. "We did all the cooking on the grill—"

"I smell something burning. We are just going to check." Chris pulled Lucy toward the house. Lucy threw her burger on her plate and stumbled along behind Chris, firmly in her grasp. Once they were inside, Chris yanked the door shut.

"Geez, you can be such a brute!"

"Do not tell Mike. Nothing is going on. She needed a job done and I needed the work. That's all!"

"Just tell him that. Why does everything have to be a secret?"

"He'll get upset."

"So? He'll get over it."

"We're not telling Mike. Your grandmother is here, and her heart is just getting better. She'll get upset if she sees Mike angry, and we don't want to do that to her heart. Not now."

Lucy groaned in frustration and yanked away her arm, which had still been in Chris's grasp.

"Fine! Not this afternoon." She stuck an index finger in Chris's face. "But you will tell him that Angel Lux owns Olivia's and you've been working for her for the past almost two weeks."

Chris sighed this time. "I will tell him."

Lucy straightened her clothes, opened the door, and went back to the deck. Chris followed.

* * *

"Olivia's" was printed on top of the check moving through the printer and "Payment in Full" was printed on the bottom.

Angel, leaning on the plywood and milk crate desk, pulled the check off the printer, signed it, and walked it up the stairs to the new rooftop patio where Chris was busy watering the plants in the vertical herb garden.

Angel looked around at the rich, sealed wood decking that covered the entire rooftop. Chris had installed the bar and wait station and the pergola looked great. Someday, Angel would have grapevines covering the pergola, but that would take time. For now, the structure of the pergola provided significant shade on the hottest part of the roof and that made it a real asset.

The planters had been installed and, at Chris's recommendation, Angel had spent the extra money to install full-sized plants. They really did give the place an established look. The lush greenery was also a great contrast to the cityscape just beyond the rooftop and created the feeling of a real oasis in the city. All-weather string lights had been installed overhead along with some safety lighting on the floor and some well-placed floodlights near the stairways. Eventually, she'd move patio heaters into the space to extend the outdoor season as fall approached, but there was no rush to do that now.

Angel looked into the late evening light and imagined a night sky with a full moon, the twinkle lights mixing with the lights from the city beyond the rooftop, maybe a singer with a guitar in the corner. Drinks. Cheers. Good food. Good friends. Romantic couples lingering over the lit candles on the tables. Olivia would have approved.

"I have a licensed electrician scheduled to stop by tomorrow," Chris said.

Angel turned to face Chris, who had stepped up beside her, unnoticed.

"All the wiring is done. He just has to make the final connections per code. That will take less than an hour. This space will look a lot different at night with lights."

"Yeah. That's just what I was thinking."

"As soon as the city does the final inspection and signs off on the work, you can open the rooftop to the public for business, but not until then. I can't stress that enough. Your liability insurance won't cover the space, and the city could fine you if you allow public occupancy before the work is approved."

"How long will that take?"

"I'm hoping to get an inspector out here in a couple weeks. Until then you can only use the patio for private, unpaid events. I know you are in the middle of the dinner rush, so let me clean up a few things and I'll be out of here in a half hour or so."

"Yeah, I've got to get back to the kitchen."

Angel turned toward the stairway and Chris started picking up a few things.

"Hey," Angel said, stopping and turning back to face her. "I have a day off tomorrow. How about you come over to my apartment? I will cook a nice meal, and we'll have one last dinner together. Just as a thank-you for all of the hard work on the patio."

Chris rubbed her hand over her face for a moment, covering her mouth.

Angel moved to fill the silence. "I know that's not strictly professional."

Angel shuffled a bit, waiting for a reply, fairly confident she would be rejected, but then she saw Chris's posture relax and her hand dropped away from her face. She smiled at Angel softly and, much to Angel's surprise, said, "I'd love that."

CHAPTER TWELVE

Angel tapped her chin while considering the finishing touches on the table. Candles were on the table, but those were too romantic. This was just a thank-you dinner, not a date. The small bouquet of flowers seemed appropriate for a dinner between friends...but maybe too much for just business associates? Angel whisked the candles off the table and moved the flowers to the bedroom. She fussed with the silverware on the table, making sure it was spot free, and pressed a fold down on one of the cloth napkins. When she was done, she nodded her approval; she always liked a table that was well set.

Dinner was smelling delicious in the kitchen, and she knew that would go smoothly. Under her well-used apron she was wearing khaki slacks and a white, collared, sleeveless blouse. Casual was the theme for dinner, she had decided, but not too casual.

She heard a car pull up on the street and went to look out the window. Chris's beat-up Subaru was already parked in front of the building across the street. The driver side door opened, and Angel watched a long, lean leg extend from the car. Chris stepped out into the evening sunlight wearing a light summer dress and low heels. Then she turned around and bent back into the car, reaching to get something.

An involuntary groan squeezed out of Angel's throat at the sight of Chris's backside as her torso went into the car. It really was a shame: this was probably the last time she'd get treated to that view.

Angel moved away from the window, checked her lipstick in a mirror by the front door, and undid another button on her blouse. Then she licked the pad of her thumb and smoothed down the wild tuft on her brow. She stepped out of her apartment and headed for the security door.

Angel opened the door in time to see Chris step onto the front porch of the building. She looked up at Angel and grinned. She held up a small bouquet of flowers and extended them to Angel. Angel smiled.

Dinner was simple but exquisite. After Chris's flowers were properly arranged in a vase on the table, Angel set out a whipped goat cheese served with baked figs. The main course was lobster and angel hair pasta, drizzled with olive oil and lemon and topped with some fresh basil from the new vertical herb garden on the rooftop. For dessert they had a creamy panna cotta with a passion fruit topping. All of it went very well with a light rosé Angel had been saving for a special occasion.

Chris ate Angel's cooking with gusto and then leaned back in the chair with her hands on her belly and a look of intense satisfaction on her face.

Angel grinned at her expression and reached over to pour a little more wine in her glass. "How about we chat in the living room for a while? It's more comfortable."

Chris nodded and they walked together into the living room, each carrying a wineglass and Angel carrying a half-full bottle of rosé. Chris climbed onto a soft, overstuffed couch behind a low coffee table, kicking off her heels, and tucking her feet underneath her bottom. Angel moved to the other end of the couch, taking off her shoes as well, and set the bottle on a nearby end table.

"That meal was amazing. You are an incredible cook. I wish I had skills like that!"

"This from the woman who single-handedly built an entire rooftop patio, custom cedar planters, a custom wait station and bar, a custom vertical garden, *and a pergola* and got it all wired up for lighting in two weeks. And you're the one who wishes you had skills!"

Chris grinned. "Yeah, that is pretty impressive, isn't it!"

"Yes. It is." Angel took a sip from her glass. "Olivia would have loved that rooftop."

Chris took a sip, too, and looked down at the floor, like she was contemplating a thought. Then she looked up at Angel. "Tell me about Olivia."

Angel took another, bigger drink of wine. She took a heavy breath into her lungs and let it out slowly.

"Olivia...was your wife," Chris continued softly.

Angel was still for a moment and then nodded. She lifted her eyes to look at Chris and smiled uncomfortably. She waited for the knots that often hit her stomach when she talked about her wife, but the knots seemed to be staying away. Chris sat in patient silence, and Angel decided she could talk about it.

She looked at the end table next to her and scanned the framed photographs there. She spied the one at the beach at sunset with her and Olivia and Babe, their big, goofy, old lab at the time. She and Olivia had their arms around each other, and Babe had managed to push her gray muzzle into the picture in front of them, her tongue lolling out of her head and happy eyes clouded by age looking right into the camera lens. Babe's antics had caused Olivia to break out in laughter just as Angel snapped the selfie. All three of them looked completely joyful and so utterly carefree at the time. Angel couldn't believe she ever had felt like that. She remembered that day on the beach but couldn't recall what those feelings were like. But here was the photographic record, with the ear-to-ear grin on her face that proved that she, indeed, had been joyful and carefree not so long ago.

She leaned over, picked up the framed photo, and reached across the couch to hand it to Chris. She set her glass down and took the picture in both hands to give it a good look. She giggled at the faces in the picture.

"You look so happy!"

"That's me, Olivia and Babe, taken a year before she died—so about six years ago." Angel cleared her throat. "I'm a widow."

Chris's smile fell and she looked up from the picture at Angel. Sadness filled her hazel gaze. "I'm so sorry."

Angel nodded an acknowledgment of her sentiment.

Chris leaned over to hand the picture back to Angel. "She was beautiful."

"She was." Angel took the picture back and gazed at the faces looking into the camera. Then she put the photograph back on the table, carefully angling it on its spot.

"Olivia was the real cook. I handled the business side of things. I helped out in the kitchen. I still do. If we need a line cook or a runner, busser, waitstaff, prep cook, bartender, I will step in. Heck, I'll wash dishes if that's what Olivia's needs on a particular night. Don't get me wrong, I can hold my own in the kitchen, but I don't have the kind of talent it takes to make a restaurant take off. Olivia had that. Since she's been gone, I've had to hire my talent. It hasn't been easy, but I've been lucky."

"Olivia's Café must be around four years old?"

"Three."

"Three. So, she never saw it."

"No. It was her dream, though. That we'd sell the food truck and start our own restaurant. I was perfectly happy with the truck, but she always wanted to…'settle down,' that's what she called it. 'Settle down.' Get a brick-and-mortar place somewhere. But we never had the money. Until she died. Then the wrongful death settlement came in and it was a good chunk of change. Of course, most of it went to pay medical bills and debts we had acquired when she couldn't work because she was so sick and I couldn't work because she needed so much care. And the lawyers! The lawyers got a big chunk. But finally, it was over and there was a big pot of money left, so I decided to use it to build Olivia her restaurant."

"She was so young when she died."

"She had just turned thirty. She was so young that none of the doctors thought she could possibly have cancer. That's probably why they missed it. Repeatedly. Plus, a test result got misplaced. And an MRI was left unread. Just sloppy, stupid mistakes that kept piling up. Until finally we saw a doctor who was like, 'Oh my god!' and got her in for radiation that day! And then surgery a week later, and then extremely aggressive chemotherapy. The chemo was horrible. Absolutely horrible! But it was too late by then. She lasted six months after the diagnosis, ovarian cancer, and that was it. She was gone."

Chris moved to sit closer to Angel on the couch. "That's so very sad. I am so very sorry for you. I can't imagine how horrible it would be to lose your wife."

Angel drained her wineglass and put it on the coffee table. It was certainly sad, but that wasn't the emotion that had overwhelmed her for the last five and a half years. What had really engulfed Angel since Olivia got sick was utter and absolute fury.

It was infuriating that the doctors had messed up so badly. Infuriating that the insurance company had put barriers in front of proper treatment. Infuriating that their one source of income, the truck, had to be sold to pay for food and a roof over their heads and the insanely increasing medical bills. Infuriating that the hospital lawyers had tried every dirty trick they could to avoid a proper payout, including arguing, frivolously, that their Canadian marriage wasn't legal in the US under Obergefell. And the most infuriating of all, that a kind, beautiful, wonderful, amazing woman like Olivia had to suffer and die at just thirty years old.

All that anger had fueled Angel's fight, first against the doctors to get a diagnosis and treatment, and then against the cancer, and then, when those fights were lost so horribly her next fight was against the malpractice insurance company and the lawyers. The court battle ended in a split decision with Angel leaving a lot of money on the table to settle the dispute instead of letting it drag on for years. But after that Angel rallied and her final fight for the restaurant had been a big win. That's where all her efforts had really been focused over the last four years.

She had buried herself in the work, laboring fourteen hours a day, seven days a week, to build the kind of restaurant Olivia had always talked about. She'd hired the people Olivia had mentioned she'd like at her dream restaurant, luring them away from their previous employers with promises of good pay and good working conditions, promises which she had kept, even when it meant she hadn't been able to pay herself and struggled to pay her own rent.

She hadn't started Olivia's with the intention of making any money at all. If the restaurant had folded and she had blown all the settlement money on a failed business—that would have been fine with her. She had just built it for Olivia and Olivia was gone anyway.

But the restaurant had thrived and was turning a healthy profit by only its second year. And by this year, going on to its fourth, it was doing a roaring business. Jasper had been an excellent head chef and her sharp management skills had kept the operation running smoothly. Olivia's vision of what the city was lacking in the restaurant scene had been spot-on, and it was no longer a fight to keep the doors open.

For years, the fury Angel felt had been like an opponent's unrelenting knee on her chest, forcing her to fight to breathe and struggle to stay alive. And now, as she sat on the couch, her bare feet comfortably curled under her, full from a good dinner, excellent wine, and lovely conversation, watching beautiful Chris as she looked curiously at the other pictures placed around the room, searching for Olivia's face in them, Angel realized that the knee on her chest was gone. When had it left? Would it be back?

Realizing she could breathe again, Angel closed her eyes and inhaled deeply through her nose, expanding her rib cage, pushing her diaphragm as far down into her stomach as she could make it go, moving air into corners of her lungs that she felt hadn't experienced oxygen in years. And then she exhaled what felt like six years of fury, expelling it into the ether, where it vaporized like a comet blinking out in the night sky.

She opened her eyes and saw Chris's keen hazel gaze focused intensely upon her. Chris picked up her wineglass from the coffee table and lifted it into the air.

"To Olivia. I wish I had known her."

Angel smiled. "You would have loved Olivia. Everybody did."

They clinked glasses and drank. Chris drained her wineglass, then reached forward to put her empty glass on the coffee table. She groaned.

"What's wrong?"

"Ugh! Moving those plants yesterday. I am feeling them this evening. I can barely lift my arms."

"You know what's great for that? I have a whirlpool tub. The jets are fantastic on sore muscles."

"What? Take a bath in your tub?"

"I'll get the water started, and we can chat some more while it fills. You can get that soreness worked out before you go, while I clean up the kitchen. What do you think of a hot bath in a jetted tub for those sore arms?"

Chris's eyes fluttered closed, and she seemed to melt a little.

"That looks like a yes," Angel said. She bounded off to get the bath started.

CHAPTER THIRTEEN

Chris found herself standing, a full glass of wine in her hand, in front of a hot, steamy bath in a large tub in somebody else's bathroom. A fluffy bath towel had been placed on the corner of the tub and the air was well scented by the whirlpool bath oil Angel had carefully dripped in the water. Cedar and orange. The smell brought her back to the moment at Chef John's restaurant when she had smelled the scent on Angel's skin, just before she had invited her back to her apartment for sex. Chris shook her head to clear that thought from her brain. That was before they had agreed to be platonic.

Taking a bath in somebody else's tub seemed like a complete breach of normal social protocol, especially when one could hear the owner of said tub clanking dishes in the kitchen as she cleaned up the wonderful meal for which she had just done all the cooking. But Chris's little apartment only had a shower and no tub at all. It had literally been years since she had sunk down in a hot bath in a real tub, much less a spacious whirlpool tub.

Chris tried to resist getting into the tub one last time but, out of curiosity, thought she'd flip the switch to turn on the jets to see what kind of power they could generate. Once the water in the tub began to froth and bubble like a giant pot in Olivia's kitchen, her aching muscles screamed for the promised relief. She couldn't hold out any longer.

She set her wineglass down on the ledge of the tub and slipped off the summer dress she was wearing and her slight underthings, letting them drop to the floor. Her shoes had long since been abandoned, she couldn't remember where.

She climbed into the steamy water, descending into heaven. The deep tub allowed her long frame to slide under the dancing waterline completely and with room to spare. She braced her toes into the far wall of the tub and sank down low, dipping down until the jetted bubbles frolicked on her chin just below her bottom lip. Jets pounded her calves and her quads, her obliques, biceps, and deltoids. Her whole body cheered after the abuse she had put it through the last couple of weeks. But it was the muscles in her back, the ones aching from carrying joists and beams and pushing wheelbarrows full of dirt and plants, not to mention the endless decking boards that had to be placed one after another bent over on hands and knees, that had been screaming the loudest. Her back desperately needed relief, and the jets behind her offered exactly that.

She positioned herself to get just the right angle from the spewing currents and in just the right locations. When she got everything arranged as she wanted it, she closed her eyes, sighed deeply, and released herself to the luxurious sensation. She stayed in that position for a while, eyes closed, letting the jets work their magic on her poor muscles, feeling the tightness in them melt away into the hot, steamy water. Thanks to the hot water, the jets, and the wine, she felt more relaxed than she had since she couldn't remember when.

Chris pulled her cut hand out of the water and examined it. Pink, fresh skin was already growing over the cut, and the liquid bandage she had applied was doing a perfect job keeping the injury sealed. Remembering the wine, she lazily scooched up a bit to get her chin and shoulders out of the water and lifted a heavy arm to grab the glass on the edge of the tub. When the stem of the glass slipped in her hand, cold wine dumped onto the hot skin of her shoulder, the glass splashed into the water, and Chris let out an involuntary yelp.

A quiet knock followed momentarily. "Chris? Everything okay?"

Chris fished around in the giant tub for the glass, hoping to God it hadn't broken and ruined her bath. "I dropped the wineglass in the tub."

"If there is broken glass in the tub, you need to turn off the—"

"I found it!" Chris triumphantly lifted the undamaged glass out of the water. "Not broken. It's fine."

"Sounds like you need some more wine," Angel said through the door. "It's part of the whole decadent experience."

As she struggled to replace the glass on the tub ledge, Chris thought that she probably had had enough wine. The glass was slippery from the water and bath oil, and she almost dropped it again. Instead of arguing with the suggestion, she decided to just focus on getting it to the ledge safely.

There was another knock on the door. "Coming in with another glass of wine."

The door opened and Angel entered with a full glass in one hand and her eyes closed. Chris shyly sunk down low into the tub, where her nakedness was obscured by the churning water. Angel laughed as she fumbled for the door handle to close the door and keep the steamy heat in the room.

Stepping away from the door, she put her free hand over her eyes and carefully made her way to the tub, holding up the full wineglass. "Maybe a plastic cup would have been a better idea."

Chris giggled as Angel blindly made her way across the spacious bathroom. "The table service is excellent at this establishment."

Angel grinned and reoriented herself to the sound of Chris's voice, moving closer with the wine. "And how's the seating, ma'am? Do you approve?"

Chris lifted her hand out of the water to reach in the direction of the wineglass as Angel got closer. "I think I must have the best seat in the house."

She grabbed Angel's hand as she reached out with the hand that had been covering her eyes, keeping her eyes closed. Chris guided her to the tub, and she carefully, slowly, sat down on the ledge.

"Yes, you have a lovely..." Angel bit her lip and paused for a moment, "...seat." She slowly opened her eyes and focused on Chris, who was still holding her hand.

Chris gazed into her beautiful blue, thickly lashed eyes, marveling at the kindness and warmth she saw in them. She looked at Angel's delicious mouth and beautiful smile. At the buttons that strained to contain the breasts underneath her white blouse. The smile dropped from her mouth and her breath started to quicken. She ignored the glass of wine Angel was holding out to her and instead gave her hand a gentle tug.

Angel's look grew serious for a moment and then sad. Her attention turned to the glass in her hand. "But you're engaged to David. I don't think I can–"

"No."

Angel's eyes bounced up from the glass to meet hers. "What?"

"I'm not...There isn't..." Unable to hold her gaze, Chris looked down at the water. "There is no David anymore."

She looked nervously up at Angel.

Angel paused to look deeply into her eyes. Then she took a large gulp of wine from the glass and set it on the tub ledge. "Are you sure about that?"

Chris nodded slowly, nervousness easing out of her body and being replaced by a sensation of pure desire. "Very sure." She released Angel's hand.

Angel leaned back and regarded her carefully. Then she reached over to the switch for the jets and turned them off. The frothing, bubbling water eased to a quick swirl, then settled down to as still as glass and the water's visibility shifted from completely opaque to crystal clear. The water level lowered with the lack of agitation.

Chris sucked in a deep breath and held it, knowing she was completely exposed. Angel's gaze lowered to Chris's mouth and then to her throat above the water. And then to her shoulders below the water level, and then her breasts, where her eyes lingered for a moment. And then down her torso to the patch between her legs, where her eyes lingered longer. And then slowly down her long thighs and all the way to Chris's toes and then back up again to lock onto Chris's eyes. Chris trembled despite the heat of the water.

Angel reached for the far tub ledge to brace herself and leaned in to give Chris a deep, searching kiss, which she reciprocated. She reached up to put her hands on Angel's waist, the water on her hands dampening Angel's shirt until she could feel the heat from her skin under the soaked fabric.

Suddenly, Angel's hand slipped on the wet tub ledge, and she lost her balance. She yelped as she began to fall, but Chris's strong arms were already under her, holding her up while she regained her grip on the tub.

Chris smiled up at the startled expression on Angel's face. "Join me. But don't fall on me this time."

Angel smiled back at Chris. She straightened herself back up on the tub ledge and reached to pull her shirt, now dripping wet from where Chris had held her, off over her head. She tossed the shirt on the floor. She reached behind herself to unlatch her bra and stripped that off as well, revealing generous, pert breasts and rosy nipples. Standing up, she undid the button and zipper of her pants and let them drop to the tile floor, clad in just a pair of lacy black panties. Chris's breath came quickly in anticipation. Her heart skipped a beat. Angel hooked her thumbs on the panties and dropped them to the floor, kicking them to the side. Confident and graceful, and without an ounce of shyness, she stepped into the warm water and slid into Chris's waiting arms.

They kissed longingly and searchingly with hot, quick breaths and exploring tongues. Angel moved to kiss Chris's ear and then to trace kisses down her neck. Chris groaned as she involuntarily arched her back. Water sloshed against the sides of the tub with her movement.

Chris began to ache at the feel of Angel's tongue on her skin, the feel of her breasts pressed into her own, and the feel of her thigh lowered between her legs.

Angel lifted off Chris slightly and looked into her eyes. "I know things got pretty heavy between us in the office, but have you been with women before? Are you comfortable with touching another woman, or would you like to take this slow?"

Chris was silent for a moment, unsure of how to respond.

Angel continued, "Just tell me what you like. And if I'm doing something you're not into, all you have to do is let me know."

Chris nodded, reached up, and wrapped an arm around Angel's waist. As the water sloshed up the sides of the tub, vigorously this time, she rolled Angel over until Angel was settled underneath her in the water. Angel reached around and cupped her bottom in her hands, giving Chris a healthy squeeze as a grin spread across her face.

Chris's voice was so low and filled with desire that she barely recognized it as her own. "I've had sex with women before." Actually, she had never had sex with men. "And what I'd really like is to kiss every square inch of your body. But I can't breathe underwater and I'm not ready to get out of this tub just yet, so what I'd like to do is caress you." Just so it was clear, she added, "Intimately."

Angel smiled. "I'd like that."

Chris leaned down to kiss her on her neck and the part of her shoulder that was above the water. Angel closed her eyes and parted her legs as Chris arranged herself, pressed against Angel's side in the confines of the tub, now tight with two people instead of one.

She slid her hand down to Angel's breast, which she cupped against her palm and massaged gently, her hand slipping over her skin through the water. Then she rolled her nipple in her fingers until it came to a hard, tight point. Angel groaned.

Chris moved her hand down to Angel's stomach, where she let her thumb drop into her shallow navel while she took some time to kiss and suck the shell of her ear. Angel reached up, took the hand on her stomach, and pulled it lower until Chris's palm was between her legs.

"I don't want to wait any longer," Angel said huskily. She released Chris's hand, moving her arms up to brace herself against the sides of the tub.

Chris's searching fingers moved through Angel's folds and the distinctive slickness there, separate from the water. Her index finger found Angel's erect clit, and Angel gasped. She settled her tongue on the pounding pulse on Angel's throat as she began to move her fingers in slow, gentle strokes over the hard, sensitive nub.

Angel groaned at the sensation, her head settling on the ledge of the tub. The water began to slosh back and forth rhythmically with Chris's movements. Her breathing became ragged. "Faster."

Chris gently bit and kissed Angel's neck and began to increase the speed of her strokes.

"Like that," Angel panted. "Keep it like that." Chris obliged, kissing and sucking and stroking as water slapped against the sides of the tub and slopped over the top. Angel arched her back again and clutched at Chris's sides and finally cried out and shuddered in release.

Chris kissed Angel's ear as she struggled to catch her breath.

"Again," Angel said desperately between gasps.

Chris complied. In just minutes she had Angel at the precipice again. She cried out as she flew over the top once more, clutching Chris's back.

After a third time, when Angel was finally spent and had a minute to catch her breath, she looked at Chris smiling above her. Angel smiled back and reached up to stroke her cheek. "What can I do for you?"

Chris thought for a moment. "The water is getting a little cool. Can we go to your bed?"

"Of course."

They opened the drain. Angel got out of the tub first. She dried off with the fluffy towel and wrapped it around herself before going into the hallway and returning with another towel. As the water level in the tub continued to lower, Chris stood. Angel took her hand to help her out, and she wrapped herself up in the towel. Angel led her into the hallway, which was lit with a night-light, the late summer sun having given way to the night while they were in the tub.

Angel led Chris to the bedroom, barely lit from the small light in the hall. There, in the darkness, with her toes curled into the thick carpet, she heard, rather than saw, Angel pull back the comforter and top sheet of the bed, releasing the smell of clean linen into the room. She and Angel took a moment to kiss passionately and then dropped their towels and climbed into the soft, cool bed.

Angel pulled the covers back over them both and moved on top of Chris. She kissed her lips, her ear, and her neck. She trailed kisses down her throat to the divot between her collarbones. She moved lower to kiss her breasts and to tongue her nipples.

Chris tented the top sheet and comforter over her knees as Angel moved lower still to kiss her flat stomach, then past her navel, and then farther down—until she got to the patch between Chris's legs, where she kissed Chris deeply. Chris shuddered at the sensation of her lips and tongue caressing her most intimate place.

"I want you inside me," Chris told her. Angel obliged, gently inserting one finger and then two. "Now kiss me," Chris said, taking Angel's face in her hands and drawing her back up to kiss her on the mouth, tasting her own salty wetness on her lips. They kissed deeply while Angel continued her up and down strokes inside her.

"Harder," Chris gasped between kisses. Angel complied. Soon Chris threw her head back. She came powerfully and with a guttural scream. She wrapped her arms around Angel to steady herself as post-climactic convulsions throbbed through her body and quickly eased. Angel lay down on the bed beside her and they curled up in each other's arms. Angel kissed her cheek and the corner of her mouth and stroked her hair as Chris struggled to catch her breath.

When Chris's breathing had finally eased, Angel curled into her side and, wordlessly, they held each other tight. Finally, Angel rolled onto her back, extending an arm to invite Chris into the crook at her left shoulder. Chris tucked herself in beside her, resting her head on her breast and her hand on her stomach over the sheet, feeling the rise and fall of her abdomen while she breathed, and smelling the cedar and orange bath oil on her skin. Angel bent the arm under Chris to draw slow, lazy circles with her short nails over her shoulder and arm and back.

Chris sighed, feeling sexually satiated, safe, and relaxed. In moments she was swallowed up by a deep, peaceful sleep.

A gentle, fresh summer breeze fluttered through the sheer bedroom curtains, allowing the morning sunshine to dapple the room and fall onto Chris's face. The sounds of birds singing and light traffic on the residential street drifted into her consciousness. She blinked at the sunlight reflected on the white walls and the white sheets on the bed. A big, blue comforter was scrunched in a pile on the carpeted floor.

Chris stretched her long, bare limbs under the cool, thin top sheet and dug her heels into the soft, luxurious cushion of a mattress of a much better quality than her own. Because she wasn't in her bed. She was in Angel's, she remembered.

Instantly, she was awake. She blinked her eyes a couple of times to get the blurriness out and looked at the other side of the bed. Empty. She checked under the sheet. Yep. Completely naked. She couldn't even remember where her clothes were.

Ah, the tub. She closed her eyes and deeply inhaled the faint smell of cedar and orange in the room. She stretched again in satisfaction at the memory of making Angel come repeatedly in the tub, of the taste of Angel's mouth, and the feeling of Angel inside her, making her world explode.

"Good morning," came a voice at the door. Chris opened her eyes to see Angel smiling in the doorway. "Do you always wake up with a smile on your face like that?"

"On special mornings."

She noticed Angel was wearing a fluffy bathrobe and holding a tray with two coffees and a plate of steaming fresh croissants and a little jar of homemade raspberry preserves.

Chris grinned at her and stretched her long limbs again. "Déjà vu. The table service here is excellent."

Angel grinned. "Déjà vu?" She walked over to the bed with the tray. "Ah. *Je pense que vous me demandez à nouveau de vous faire l'amour.*"

"Oh, I don't know what you said, but that sounds so sexy!"

"How about some breakfast?"

Chris nodded enthusiastically. Angel walked over and climbed into the bed with the tray and set it between them. She gingerly opened one of the hot croissants and smeared on some jam and handed it to Chris before doing her own.

Chris gratefully started to eat. "Say something else in French," she said between bites.

"Something else?" Angel licked raspberry off her lips. "*J'ai mis la confiture dans un pot pour qu'elle ait l'air maison mais je l'ai achetée dans un magasin.* Is that sexy?"

Chris leaned in for a passionate kiss, which Angel reciprocated. When they parted, she said, "Yeah. That's sexy."

Angel smiled and took a sip of her coffee. She did the same. "How did you learn French?"

"My wife taught me, sort of. She grew up speaking French and English in Montreal and when she got angry with me, she would curse me out in French, so I had to learn what she was saying."

"How'd you manage that?"

"I'd record her on my phone and send it through an online translator."

Chris giggled, taking another sip of her coffee.

"I did!" Angel took another bite of croissant. "The online translators are a lot better now than they used to be, let me tell you! It worked good enough. I used a hard copy French-to-English dictionary for the stuff that wouldn't go through the translator. But for a long time, my entire French vocabulary was just curse words. Eventually, I figured out a little more."

Chris put the last bite of her croissant in her mouth and put her coffee down on the tray. "Teach me some French."

Angel arched her scarred eyebrow at Chris and put her coffee on the tray, moving that off of the bed and onto the nightstand next to the alarm clock. She picked up Chris's hand and lifted the palm to her mouth.

"*Puis-je vous embrasser la main, madame?*" said Angel.

"What did you say?" asked Chris, her eyelids lowering and her voice growing husky at Angel's tone.

Angel looked up at her. "May I kiss your hand, madame?"

Chris nodded. "Yes."

"*Oui,*" said Angel.

"*Oui,*" repeated Chris.

Angel kissed her palm. "*La main.*"

"*La main,*" repeated Chris.

Angel lifted the inside of Chris's elbow to her mouth and again looked up at her. "*Puis-je embrasser ton bras, madame?*"

"Arm?" asked Chris.

Angel nodded and hovered her lips over the pulse that thumped at the inside bend of the elbow. "*Ton bras.*"

"*Ton bras. Oui,*" said Chris.

Angel kissed the bend of Chris's elbow. Then Angel gently brushed her locks from her shoulder and trailed kisses slowly up Chris' arm. "*Puis-je embrasser ton épaule?*"

Chris's breath quickened and her eyes closed as she absorbed the sensation of Angel's lips and tongue on her skin. "*Ép… épaule. Oui.*"

Angel kissed Chris's shoulder and then moved in to kiss her neck. "*Puis-je vous embrasser le cou, madame?*" Angel's hand dropped to Chris's breast and she gently began to caress it. "*J'adore ton cou.*"

"*J'adore…*" Chris's head started to swim. "*J'adore ton…*"

Angel moved her mouth to mere centimeters from Chris. "*Ton cou,*" She left her lips in the "ooo" shape.

"Cooooo." Chris panted, trembling from the heat of Angel's hand on her breast. She closed her eyes and bent her head back as Angel moved in even closer.

"*Mais je dois aller travailler*," Angel breathed over her.

"*Mais je... ah...*Huh?" Chris opened her eyes and saw Angel had moved away and was looking at her sadly.

"*Mais je dois aller travailler.* I have to go to work. I'm scheduled to do some inventory this morning."

"Oh," said Chris. Her bottom lip popped out in a pout.

Angel laughed and kissed the pout. "Guess I'll schedule inventory for another day. Good thing I'm the boss."

* * *

Chris woke up for the second time that day and checked the clock on the nightstand. One p.m. Christ! How many hours had she slept today?

"Good afternoon." Angel was standing in the doorway, fully dressed and showered this time, and holding a tray with a couple of cups of coffee and a plate of something hot and toasty.

Chris grinned at her and stretched. "Good afternoon. Déjà vu again!"

"Déjà vu again, indeed!" Angel walked over and set the tray on the bed between them and climbed on top of the covers.

Chris looked hungrily at the sandwich on the plate. "I love grilled cheese sandwiches!" She looked at them a little more closely. "These look a lot better than mine."

"Goat cheese and pear."

Chris reached hungrily for a triangle and took a bite. She happily nodded her approval and Angel took the other triangle and started to eat.

Chris licked some pear juice off her lip. "I should thank you."

"Thank me for what?"

"Thank you for the French lesson this morning."

"You enjoyed that?"

"I did. I wish I could teach you something."

Angel sipped her coffee. "Well, maybe you could teach me something about carpentry."

"Carpentry isn't very sexy."

Angel's eyes twinkled. "Try me."

"What? Like, do you want to see my biscuit joiner?"

"Mmm," Angel purred, setting down her coffee. "I think I'd love to see your biscuit joiner," she said suggestively. "Say something else."

Chris giggled. "I need a new set of...thrust bearings. Maybe you could help me pick some out online."

Angel leaned into her neck and growled behind her ear. "I know a really hot website I could show you where they sell lots of interesting...machinery and...other equipment, including thrust bearings."

Chris set her half-eaten sandwich down on the tray. "Then after we get those, I'll teach you how to counterbore a screw so you can get it in nice and deep."

Angel sat up and looked directly at Chris. A smile tugged at the corner of Chris's mouth and she gave a sly wink.

Angel groaned. "This is so much fun! But I must get to work. I have to go in for a shift today. I'm on the schedule."

"But you're the boss, remember? Maybe you could adjust your schedule a little?" Chris timidly tucked some loose locks behind her ear. "Be an hour late, maybe?"

Angel smiled. "After last night, you still want to...?"

She nodded.

"And this morning?"

She nodded.

Angel sighed heavily and climbed off her and the bed. "The staff are expecting me."

"Fifteen minutes," negotiated Chris, letting the sheet drop away from her shoulder to expose a bare breast.

Angel's eyelids grew heavy as she watched the sheet fall away, but then she looked at the time on the clock and frustratedly ran a hand through her hair.

"Five minutes," said Chris, blushing, pulling the luxurious white sheet off the rest of her naked body and opening up her legs. "I really just need five minutes, max."

Angel grinned widely. "Five minutes. I guess I have time for that." She jumped back on the bed.

CHAPTER FOURTEEN

"So, I told Margaret that if she thought she was going to jam the copy machine again after I just said that the envelope feeder wasn't working that would be the last straw! It's just another way she keeps undermining me."

Chris dreamily rubbed a piece of sandpaper over the slab at the shop while Lucy yammered away in a chair behind her.

"Hey, you're not listening to me!"

"No, I'm listening. Undermining you."

Lucy squinted at the sly smile at the corner of Chris's mouth. Her eyes widened with realization. "You got laid!"

Chris rolled her eyes, disgusted at her own obviousness.

Lucy hopped off the workbench she was sitting on and hurried to stand over her. "What's her name? What does she do? How long have you been seeing each other? Do I know her? Most importantly, how good is she in bed?" Lucy grabbed Chris's shoulder and pulled her around to face her. "Forget that last question. From that goofy look on your face I'd say she's an astounding lay!"

Chris put the sandpaper down. "She's nobody you know, and I don't want to—"

"Wait. How would you have any time to see anybody? You've been working night and day putting in that patio for…"

Chris started to fidget under Lucy's scrutiny.

Lucy's eyes went wide again. "Oh, my god! You're fucking the seductress!"

Chris shook her hands in frustration. "She's not…It's not like that."

Lucy arched her eyebrows. "You're not fucking her?"

She stepped away from Lucy and the slab and started nervously redoing her ponytail. Lucy was right behind her.

"What about that woman at work who has been undermining you?" asked Chris.

"What about her? Fuck her. Tell me about Angel Lux. You told me and Maddie that nothing was going on between you two. That you just needed the work while Mike was out."

"That was true…" Chris paused, "… at the time."

"So, there's something going on between you now?"

Chris sighed deeply and Lucy moved in close and waited. She took another breath. "We had sex."

"Oh, I knew it!" Lucy howled, grasping her hands and pulling her to the bench to sit down together. "When?"

"Just last night."

"Uh-huh."

"And this morning."

"Yeah?"

"And this afternoon. We had a lot of sex."

Lucy squealed. "Tell me! Tell me! Was it good?"

"Soooo good!"

"Yeah?"

"Like, mind blowing." She made a motion with her hands to indicate her head exploding and she added an accompanying sound.

"No wonder Maddie couldn't resist. And Maddie's straight!" Lucy looked Chris up and down. "It was a mistake sending you in. I knew it should have been me. I'm the one who should have gotten laid last night. And this morning. And this afternoon. Damn, woman!" Lucy gave her another once-over. "There was no way you could resist that seductress's charms."

"Hey, maybe she didn't seduce me. Maybe I seduced her!"

"Yeah. How do we figure that one out?" Lucy swished her hands in the air. "Doesn't matter. So how do we tell Mike you are dating Angel Lux?"

Chris stepped away. "Well, I don't know if we are dating yet."

"Tell me again how the sex was with her."

"It was amazing!"

"Did she like it?"

"I'd say, yes, she seemed to like it a lot."

"Do you want it to be a one-time thing?"

Chris paused. Of course, she knew the answer. It was just hard to say. "No. I don't want it to be a one-time thing."

"So Mike should be told."

"We should not tell Mike."

"No. *We* aren't telling Mike."

"Right."

"*You* are telling Mike."

"No."

"Yes."

"No!"

Just then Lucy's phone rang. She gave Chris a sidelong glance, letting her know this conversation was not over, and pulled the phone out of her purse. She looked at the name of the caller on the screen.

"It's Maddie." Lucy tapped the answer button on her phone. "Hi, Maddie. Sorry, I can't talk right now. Chris and I—"

Lucy went silent.

Chris's phone dinged to indicate an incoming text message. She pulled the phone out of her pocket and scanned the short message.

Lucy's eyes widened. "Mike is *where*?"

Chris looked up at Lucy from the text message. "It's Angel. She says it's an emergency."

CHAPTER FIFTEEN

Chris parked the Subaru in a ramp not far from Olivia's, and she and Lucy jumped out of the car. Together they rushed to the restaurant.

"Slow down. I can't keep up!"

Chris slowed her pace a bit.

At Olivia's, Chris yanked open the door and held it for Lucy and then followed her inside. Lucy stopped at the maître d' station and peered around the busy dining room that rumbled with conversation from the guests. Chris spied Angel standing by the kitchen in the doorway garbed in her white and black chef's coat and black tie-back cap. She signaled them over. Chris grabbed Lucy's hand and hauled her over. Angel hurried past the kitchen crew with their clanging pots and hissing burners and headed for the office. Chris followed with Lucy in tow.

Once all three were in the little office, Angel shut the door. Chris stepped around Lucy, grabbed Angel's face, and planted a deep, hungry kiss on her mouth. Angel returned the kiss with equal gusto.

Lucy put her hands on her hips and rolled her eyes in disgust. "Okay, okay! That's enough, you two."

Angel and Chris reluctantly separated, both grinning.

Chris cleared her throat and gestured to Lucy. "Angel, this is Lucy, Mike's sister. Lucy—"

Lucy put her hands on her hips and scowled. "We've met."

Chris rubbed her chin. "Oh. At the club. I forgot."

"Hi, Lucy. How are you doing?"

"How am I doing? Well, let's see. I was supposed to be a bridesmaid in a week. But that's canceled and the bride is heartbroken about it. And my brother, the groom, he's heartbroken, too. Then my grandmother literally had her heart break and ended up in the hospital. And now this one," Lucy gestured at Chris, "is probably on her way to a heartbreak as well. And you," Lucy pointed a finger in Angel's face and squinted her eyes, "you are not responsible for only one of those."

"Okay, cool it, Lucy." Chris put a hand over Lucy's accusatory finger and gently lowered it to her side. Then Chris turned to Angel. "What's Mike doing here?"

Angel fidgeted. "I don't know, but he keeps telling the waitstaff he wants to talk to the owner. I can't believe Maddie got back together with that oaf."

Lucy glared at Angel and slammed her hand down on the plywood and milk crate desk, knocking the plywood askew. "Nobody calls my brother an oaf!"

Chris turned to Lucy. "Oh, you call your brother an oaf all of the time. What did Maddie tell you on the phone?"

"She said he told her he had a surprise for her and that he wanted to give it to her here. She tried to talk him into going somewhere else, but he insisted."

Chris turned back to Angel. "Where is he?"

Angel opened the office door and Lucy and Chris followed her to the doorway between the kitchen and the dining room. Angel nodded her head toward the dining room.

"Table twelve. It's one of the window tables to the right."

Chris and Lucy peeked out, spying the table where Mike was drinking and grinning and Maddie was fidgeting, checking her phone for texts.

Chris and Lucy leaned back into the kitchen, moving out of the way of the staff.

Chris shrugged. "They are just having dinner. He doesn't look angry or anything. Maybe it's no big deal."

"But he keeps asking for the owner. He's not still mad at me, is he?"

"Oh, he is so mad at you," responded Lucy. "Just last night he said he'd pound you into the ground if he ever got his hands on you."

Angel's eyes went wide.

Chris gruffed in annoyance. "Don't say that. You know Mike talks like that sometimes, but he's never pounded anybody."

"And I've never been pounded before, but there's always a first time."

A wicked grin crossed Lucy's face. "According to Chris, last night you two were pounding each other all night long."

"Hey, hi you two!" declared Mike cheerfully, suddenly looming in the doorway.

Chris and Lucy let out surprised yelps. Angel put a hand up to hide her face and quickly slunk into the kitchen to blend in with the other staff.

"I was headed to the men's room and I saw you guys by the kitchen here. I thought I saw you walking up the street. What are you doing here?"

"I…ah…Lucy wanted to see the patio, so I brought her over." Chris turned to Lucy. "Like I was saying, the staff entrance to the rooftop is through a stairway off the kitchen over there, but"—Chris gestured toward a closed door by the entrance—"the guests will enter through a stairway over there." Chris turned back to Lucy. "Did you like the patio?"

Lucy stood open-mouthed for a second, but then spoke. "Loved it! Gorgeous. Great patio…especially the"—Lucy smacked her lips as she thought—"patio…thing."

"Pergola," added Chris.

Lucy snapped her fingers. "Pergola! Yes."

Mike's brow furrowed in confusion. "You saw it already?" Mike pointed toward the street. "But I just saw you—"

"Glad you liked it. I'll take you home now, Lucy." Chris looped her arm through Mike's right elbow and Lucy followed suit to loop hers through his left and they started to lead him back into the dining room. "What are you doing here, big guy?"

Mike gestured to the window table where Maddie was texting on her phone frantically. Little random text message dings emanated from the phone in Lucy's purse. Chris looked at the purse and gave Lucy a sideways glance. She released Mike's arm and reached in her purse, and the phone went silent.

"I brought Maddie here because I have a surprise for her. I wanted to go somewhere romantic and Yelp suggested Olivia's, the same place you put in the rooftop deck, can you believe it? It took me two days to get a reservation. But oh my god, the beignets here are so good! Just those made it worth it. Have you tried them yet? They really are incredible! I can't stop eating them. And when the little basket is empty, they just bring more. It's amazing!"

Chris pointed to a hallway at the back of the restaurant. "The restrooms are over there by the exit sign. Now that Lucy has seen the deck, we'll get out of here and leave you to your romantic dinner with Maddie and the beignets."

Chris started to lead him toward the restrooms, but he stopped flat. She was jerked backward like she had hooked a stop sign with her arm while running.

"Hey, I want to see the rooftop, too! I've been trying to talk to the owner to get permission to go up there, but I don't know if he's not around or what. But you just showed it to Lucy." Mike turned to Chris. "You can show it to me, too!"

He quickly checked over his shoulder on Maddie and then turned back to Chris. He leaned in to quietly talk to her. Lucy leaned in over Chris's shoulder to hear. "I'm glad you're here. I wanted to talk to you about something important that involves Maddie. I tried to call you last night, but you must have had your phone turned off."

"I was busy." "She was busy." Chris and Lucy said at the same time.

"Chris has something to tell you too, Mike."

Chris subtly shook her head at Lucy, but Lucy ignored her.

"I'm going to go say hi to Maddie." And then Lucy turned and headed over to Maddie's table.

Mike nodded at Chris. "Okay, you can tell me something first." He pointed toward the bathrooms. "I just really gotta use the little boy's room first."

Chris nodded and Mike strode away. Chris rubbed her forehead in frustration.

Suddenly, Angel was at Chris's side. "What's going on?"

"Nothing. He's just taken his girl out for a romantic dinner. He doesn't know you own this place. He thinks the owner is a man, anyway."

A server stepped up to Angel and handed her an empty basket. "Table twelve needs more beignets."

Angel snatched the basket from him and made a disgusted sound. "Christ almighty! How many beignets can one man eat?"

The server stepped away and she turned back to Chris. "So, we'll just serve them dinner and they'll leave."

"He wants to see the rooftop."

Angel stiffened.

"He's my business partner," Chris interrupted before Angel could start arguing. "He wants to see my work. It will just take a couple of minutes."

Angel narrowed her eyes at Chris.

"I already told him I was here to show the rooftop to Lucy, so he won't understand if I won't show it to him."

Angel let loose a few choice words in French and then finished with, "Fine. But you'll owe me."

Chris smiled slyly. "I'll pay you back, I promise."

Angel quickly glanced around to check if anyone was watching. "Yeah, you will." She kissed Chris on the mouth and then turned and strode quickly back to the kitchen.

Chris led Mike up the customer staircase and onto the rooftop. "Eyes still closed?"

Mike's large palm was over his face. "Eyes are closed!"

Except for the floodlights at the exits, the roof was extremely dark. The sun had gone down, and only deep purples and maroons were left in the sky. A few stars were starting to pop out, barely visible in the city sky. Chris walked over to a switch box on a wall and flipped on the lights.

"Okay, open them up!"

Mike opened his eyes. The string lights twinkled overhead. Low lighting lit pathways across the deck. The vegetation in the planters and on the vertical garden swayed in the breeze, throwing shadows across the wood deck and brick walls surrounding the space. Traffic hummed on nearby streets and echoed off the buildings, punctuated by an occasional car honk here and there. City lights glinted beyond the rooftop. Wrought iron tables and chairs were set up around the deck, waiting for customers.

"Wow! This is beautiful! You did this all yourself?"

"Almost. There was a little bit of framing up, but I did most of it."

Mike began to stroll through the rooftop, looking at the features.

"Great pergola!" he said, stroking the wood on the beams and examining the construction. "Nice joins."

"Fortunately, those posts were already set."

"Those planters are pretty good sized. Must have hauled at least thirty bags of dirt up here."

"Thirty-five."

Mike jumped up and down on the decking a couple of times, watching the boards under his feet carefully. He smiled and looked back up at Chris. "Solid!"

She grinned.

Mike pointed at the custom bar and wait station. "Oooh!" He walked over to it, smiled at her again, and ran a hand across the woodwork. "Damn, girl! That's some nice carpentry!"

Her heart fluttered.

Mike walked over to the north rooftop edge and looked out at the lake illuminated by the moonlight in the distance. "Pcople are going to love this!"

She walked over to Mike and stood next to her friend while they looked at the city rooftops and moonlit lake together.

"Yelp said this place was romantic before, but wait until everybody gets a load of this!"

"I know!" Chris grinned. "Okay, better get back in. You can't leave your girl too long at the table when you are supposed to be on a romantic date."

"This is perfect for my surprise!" He turned to Chris.

"What?"

"I'm going to re-propose to Maddie! Propose again. Re-propose. Right out here on this rooftop! Under the stars."

"Mike, that's great!"

"I don't have a ring. She never took it off. I don't have anything to give her."

She plucked a strongly scented gardenia out of a planter and handed it to Mike. "Give her this."

Mike took the flower. "Can you go get her?"

She nodded.

"How do I look?" he asked, fussing with the flower stem.

Chris reached up and smoothed Mike's hair and adjusted his tie.

"Very handsome."

"Do you think she'll say yes?"

She smiled at Mike. "She'd be crazy not to."

On her way back down the stairs and through the kitchen Chris met up with Angel, who eyed her curiously.

"If you want to see the first of many proposals on your rooftop, go up and watch." Then she walked over to the table where Maddie and Lucy were chatting intensely.

CHAPTER SIXTEEN

Chris escorted Maddie and Lucy to the rooftop. They exited the customer stairway and Maddie looked around at the pretty string lights, the lush plants, solid pergola, the attractive rich wood decking, and the decorative wrought iron tables and chairs.

Then she looked up to see Mike standing in the middle of the space holding the flower. Lucy stopped and Chris kept walking with Maddie to Mike. When they got to him, Chris gave the trembling guy a thumbs-up and then retreated to stand with Lucy at a discreet distance away so as not to be able to hear their conversation. A couple of staff had filtered out and were standing quietly by the stairway to the kitchen to watch. Chris glanced over at the staff to see Angel standing behind her crew. Angel smiled at Chris and she grinned back.

Everybody watched as Mike got down on one knee and Maddie started to cry. He said some quiet words that only Maddie could hear, and he extended the flower to her. She accepted it and nodded. And then, with tears in his eyes and his face full of joy, he jumped up. His voice echoed off the city buildings as he bellowed, "She said yes!" He lifted Maddie high in the air and swung her around before setting her on her feet.

Lucy and Chris, the staff, and even some people on the street cheered. Lucy and Chris and the restaurant staff ran over to congratulate the happy couple. Somebody among the staff popped the cork from a champagne bottle and soon enough glasses were passed all around and were quickly filled.

Chris's breath caught in her throat when she saw Angel, blending in with the rest of the staff in her uniform, quietly filling glasses. Angel smiled and winked at her as she discreetly filled the glass in Mike's left hand as Jasper vigorously shook his right, congratulating Mike loudly about the engagement.

Then Chris saw Angel turn to Maddie, who was watching Angel with what was probably the same look of dismay that was on Chris's face. Angel put an arm around Maddie and hugged her close and gave her a kiss on the cheek. Chris saw Angel smile and her lips say the word, "Congratulations."

Angel filled Maddie's glass and Chris watched as the concern on Maddie's face melted into fondness and she gave Angel a pretty smile.

Chris also noticed Lucy turn the charm on Jasper, smiling at him, batting her eyes, and laughing at practically every word he said. Jasper reached over and took Lucy's hand. Chris shook her head. Poor guy didn't stand a chance of resisting when the Red Reaper of Hearts had him in her sights.

Chris lifted her glass and cleared her throat to get the attention of the crowd. "Here's to forgiveness and second chances. But most of all, here's to love and to two people who clearly were meant to be together." She snuck a glance at Angel standing behind her staff. Angel smiled at Chris and lifted her glass in her direction.

"Cheers!" shouted the little crowd, and everybody drank.

Jasper let go of Lucy's hand and stepped back over to his crew. "Okay! Drink up. We've got to get back to work!"

The staff threw back their champagnes—Jo threw back two—and they started to head back into the building. Angel began collecting glasses.

Lucy walked over to Mike and Maddie and tapped her chin. "Maybe you two could shoot for a spring wedding this time."

Maddie groaned. "Oh my god, I don't want to plan another wedding!"

"Why do we have to?" asked Mike. "Let's go through with the original date."

Chris startled. "That's next Saturday, just one week away."

Maddie shook her head. "I don't know if we have enough time. We don't even have a venue."

"Hey," said Mike with a big grin on his face to Jasper as he started moving his crew into the stairway. "Who can I thank for the champagne?"

Jasper pointed at Angel. "The owner. Angel Lux."

Angel, holding a platter full of empty champagne glasses, looked at Mike and froze. Chris and Maddie gasped, and Lucy spit champagne all over a half dozen decking boards. Maddie, Lucy, Chris, and Angel watched as the grin on Mike's face slowly disappeared and his expression grew dark. He drew up to his full six-foot six-inch height. His eyes narrowed into slits. His brow lowered ominously, and the muscles in his jaw bulged as he clenched his teeth. His face and neck flushed. His eyes moved to follow the direction Jasper was pointing, and when he saw Angel a big, purple vein popped out on his forehead and his stare fixed upon her like a predator. He set his glass down on a table.

Chris turned to Angel. Without taking her eyes off Mike, Angel handed the tray of glasses to Jasper as he walked by. Chris saw her suck in a breath through her clenched teeth, and then Chris turned to see every muscle in Mike's body tighten, his shoulders round over, and his head come down. He started to charge toward Angel, his hands out and fingers splayed to grab her. Angel took several quick steps backward and then spun around and slammed into the wall next to the kitchen stairwell, missing the doorway by a couple of feet.

Before Chris could fill her lungs with enough air to shout his name, Mike was charging across the rooftop. Angel spun around to face him, squeezed her eyes shut, pressed herself into the wall, and braced for the pounding. Chris burst after him.

Maddie, who had started moving toward Angel before Mike had even put his drink down, was suddenly in between Mike and Angel, blocking his way.

"Mike!" she barked at him. He stopped directly in front of Maddie with Angel tucked on the floor behind her and pinned against the wall.

"Mike!" Maddie shouted louder at him. He tore his eyes off Angel's trembling frame to look down at her. Chris took up a position to her right and Lucy showed up on her left. Jasper and Jo each leaped in to grab one of Mike's arms.

Maddie put her hands up on Mike's chest. "Our wedding is in just a week. Seven days! If you get hauled off to jail tonight, I might not be able to get you out by Saturday and then we'll miss our wedding date and who knows when we'll be able to get married after that."

A few of Maddie's words seemed to sink through the thick swarm of rage emanating off him. Maddie pressed her hands harder into his chest. "Please, Mike. Let's just get married."

Chris stepped forward. "Come on, big guy. You still want to marry your girl, don't ya'?"

Mike looked at Chris and his brow furrowed in confusion; he looked as if people were talking to him in a foreign language. Finally, recognition crossed his face; he was slowly starting to understand what people were saying. His color turned a shade closer to his typical pink. He nodded, but then turned his glare toward Chris, who shuddered a bit under his imposing stare.

"You've been working for *her*!" Mike said the word "her" like it was filth in his mouth.

"It was just a job, Mike," she said calmly and soothingly.

Mike squinted his eyes suspiciously at her.

"Come on, Mike," said Maddie. "Let's get ready for the wedding."

Mike looked down into her pleading eyes, and his frame relaxed slightly. "Yeah?"

Maddie patted his chest. "The flowers and the tux are prepaid. I've got a dress. We've already got a deposit down holding the date for the photographer, the musicians, and the officiant. And we've got the rings. We can do it!"

Mike's face softened. "But we've lost the venue."

Everybody was quiet for a minute, but then Lucy stepped forward. "Well, nobody wants to say it because it's so obvious. But we can have the wedding here."

Lucy and Chris looked down at Angel, who was still crouched behind them, trapped against the wall.

No! No. No! mouthed Angel silently and desperately to the two women.

Lucy turned back to Mike. "A number of guests have already canceled their travel plans. The rest will fit fine right here on this rooftop. I'm sure Angel Lux would love to make this big gesture of apology for everything that's happened and let you have the wedding right here."

Chris watched as Angel rolled her eyes and clapped her hands over her face.

"Yeah," said Chris carefully. "Maybe she'd consider that? It might help a lot to smooth things over."

Angel slowly stood up until she was peeking between the shoulders of Maddie and the much taller Chris. Mike's countenance grew dark again at the sight of her.

"I would love to have your wedding on my rooftop," Angel croaked. "Love it! Love the idea." She cleared her throat. "Unfortunately, Chris has told me the restaurant can't use the rooftop yet because it hasn't been permitted for public occupancy. It could take weeks to get a city inspector out here, Chris has said, so it's just too bad, but—"

Mike squinted his eyes at Angel. "It can't be employed for public use. That doesn't apply to private events not intended to generate revenue."

Chris turned her head to look at Angel and nodded. It was true. Angel slouched in defeat. Then she stood up straight and lifted her head to look Mike in the eye.

"As a gesture of goodwill and as an apology for everything that's happened, I'd like to give you the use of the rooftop next Saturday for the wedding—"

"And the reception," interrupted Mike.

"—and the reception," continued Angel.

"And the meal. For free."

Angel shuddered and closed her eyes for a moment while she gathered herself again. Then she opened her eyes, stood tall and with her chin up to look almost a full foot in the air over Maddie's head, locking her stare on Mike's eyes.

"The wedding and reception. Out here. You cover the cost of the food and liquor, I'll provide the labor to prepare, serve, and clean up. And you get the use of the rooftop for free."

"What about the rehearsal dinner?" added Maddie.

Angel didn't take her eyes off Mike.

"You can have the back room Monday night, that's my slow night, but you're paying for dinner."

Angel and Mike stood for a moment, evaluating each other. Maddie, before anybody else, sensed a change in the atmosphere and stepped to the side so Mike and Angel could regard each other directly.

Suddenly, Mike relaxed. Jo and Jasper carefully let go of his arms, and he extended his right hand in Angel's direction.

"Deal," he said.

Angel put her fine hand in Mike's giant paw.

"Deal," she said and shook his hand.

Angel looked around at the eyes watching her, including Chris's. She lifted her chin, spun on her heel, and headed back to the kitchen stairway. Her staff followed as Chris, Maddie, and Lucy walked Mike back to the customer stairway.

Mike turned to Lucy and Maddie. "Let me talk to Chris."

Lucy and Maddie looked at each other and then back to Chris. She nodded. Lucy and Maddie opened the door to the stairway and went inside, and then she and Mike were on the rooftop alone.

Mike regarded her carefully, his chin firmly set. "Are you and her a thing? Is that what you wanted to tell me?"

A tremor ran through Chris. She wasn't afraid of Mike, despite his size and his temper. But if she told him the truth, worse than angry, he would be disappointed. Disappointed in her. He would believe she betrayed him. He might get over it eventually, like Lucy said, but he'd never trust her again. Chris knew she couldn't have that.

"Look, Mike, don't say anything to Lucy or Maddie about this, but I've been stringing her along. Just like the trap we planned. To keep her out of the way while you wooed Maddie back. It's worked! Okay? Nothing to worry about. We'll have the wedding and then I'll dump her, and she'll be miserable. You'll like that, won't you?"

The deep frown that had furrowed Mike's entire face suddenly lifted, and he grinned down at Chris. "You're a good friend!"

She nodded.

* * *

Angel strode confidently down the stairs to the kitchen, her agreement with the redheaded ogre made. Jasper followed her down the stairs with Jo behind him.

At the bottom of the stairs Angel turned to Jasper. "Settle up the bill with that asshole and get them out of my restaurant."

Jasper nodded and left.

Angel headed for the office but didn't quite make it, grabbing the wall and leaning into it heavily as her knees went weak.

Jo was suddenly at her side. "You okay, boss?"

She nodded, reached out, and squeezed Jo's shoulder to indicate her gratitude. "I'm fine. Back to your station."

Jo looked over Angel warily and headed back to the line.

Angel put a hand on her throbbing shoulder, the one that she had bashed trying to escape from the rooftop. She leaned into the wall behind her as her knees went wobbly again and closed her eyes. She could feel the coldness of the drywall penetrating her chef's jacket and through the thin T-shirt underneath to her back. With her eyes still closed, she let go of her shoulder and let her hands drop to her sides. She took a few deep breaths and listened to the kitchen, the chopping of knives on cutting boards, the bang of pan lids, the hiss of the gas under the burners. The sounds and smells of the kitchen began to swirl together in her head.

"Come on, beautiful. Back on your feet."

Angel's eyes snapped open, and she realized she had slid about halfway down the wall and had been headed for the floor. But now Chris was standing in front of her with her strong, capable hands wrapped around her upper arms and lifting her back up into a standing position.

"You did great out there!" Chris said with a big grin. "Everything's going to be fine now. You fixed it all!"

"That brute was going to kill me!"

"He's just scary like that because he's so big. He never would have hurt you."

"Yeah? Then why did you tell him I was just a job. Is that the truth? Maybe a job and a one-night stand? Or a night, morning, and afternoon stand?"

The irony was not lost on Angel that she, the queen of one-night stands, was feeling hurt at the possibility of being somebody else's one-night stand.

Chris cleared her throat and glanced uncomfortably in the direction of the kitchen. Angel followed her eyes to see her crew all frozen in place and staring wide-eyed at them. As her eyes landed on them, they immediately returned their attention to their stations, where they all quickly started chopping and dicing and sautéing.

Chris put an arm around Angel's waist and led her into the office. Once inside, she closed the door. Angel leaned heavily on the plywood and milk crate desk, which was still askew from when Lucy had pounded it.

Chris walked over to Angel and put a hand on her back. "You aren't a one-night stand."

Angel turned to look at her. "No? Do you want more than that?"

She nodded. "Yes."

Angel nodded, too. "So do I."

Chris put her hands on her shoulders. "Mike is really emotional right now. He has a wedding coming up, thanks to you. It just wasn't a good time to tell him. That's all."

"How long are you going to keep him in the dark?"

"Just until after the wedding. He'll be a lot less stressed after that. Then I'll tell him."

Angel lifted her hands to straighten her tie-back cap and noticed that her hands were trembling.

"Christ! I'm still shaking!" Her knees started to buckle, and she began to sink to the floor again. Chris pulled her back up.

"Look, how about I take you home, pour you a glass of wine or two, draw you a nice hot bath, and turn on the jets." Chris smiled and moved a little closer to Angel. "Then I'll massage your back, get your mind off what happened on the rooftop, and"—she leaned in to whisper in Angel's ear—"I'll help you release all that tension."

Angel scowled, considering the terrible night she was having, and then thought about how Chris could make it all so much better. She looked up into her twinkling hazel eyes. Eyes that, just for a moment, held something that looked like a pang of sadness or maybe guilt. It went away quickly, and Chris smiled at her again.

A smile tugged at the corner of Angel's mouth. She nodded. Chris took her hand, and they left the office.

CHAPTER SEVENTEEN

Chris, Lucy, and Maddie stood at the picnic table on Lucy's deck and, in assembly line fashion, worked to put together decorative centerpieces for the reception tables, the assembled pieces ending up carefully packed in boxes on the ground and set in the shade.

"Is that it? Is that the last one?" Lucy asked as the final centerpiece exited the line and Chris carefully placed it in a box. Chris did a quick count of the items in the boxes while Maddie started to clean up the table. Lucy picked up a list on a clipboard and a pen.

"Sixteen. That's all of them," Chris reported.

"Centerpieces. Check!" Lucy made a check on her list with the pen. "Rings."

Chris held up a hand. "Check! I got those!"

Lucy threw her hands out dramatically. "Oh my god! The marriage license!"

"Mike is picking that up on Friday and he is also picking up his tux." Maddie jammed her fingers in her thick, brunette hair. "There's so much to do! We lost weeks!"

"We've got it! We can do it!" Lucy pumped her fist. "We've just got to pare it down to the important stuff. It will be beautiful! A short ceremony at sunset, then a meal and then the dance. Hey, is Elizabeth Bentley still available to officiate the ceremony?"

"Thankfully, yes! I love her."

"She got rave reviews on Yelp as an event planner and wedding officiant."

"Yeah, we couldn't afford her event planning services. She is just performing the ceremony. She will be at the rehearsal dinner tonight."

Lucy, Chris, and Maddie carried the boxes packed with decorations to Chris's Subaru parked in the driveway and started stuffing them in the trunk.

"The cake?" asked Maddie.

"That was delivered to Olivia's today. They have room to keep it in the walk-in refrigerator until the wedding. Angel says it's cold enough and will keep fine." Chris carefully shoved some boxes around in the back of her car, trying to make everything fit.

"Thanks for storing this stuff at the shop. It sure takes up a lot of room."

"Yeah, no problem. I'll drop this off there and go home and change. I'll meet you guys over at Angel's restaurant for the rehearsal."

Lucy leaned against the car. "Speaking of Angel, you haven't told us yet." She looked Chris in the eye as Chris glanced uncomfortably at her. "Are you two getting serious?"

Maddie stepped closer to listen to the reply.

"Well, it's fun right now…" Chris paused, surprised at the way her heart had fluttered at the question. "…but I don't know if I'd call it serious."

Maddie glanced at the hand Chris hadn't realized she had clutched to her chest over her heart. Chris threw her hand down to her side. Maddie's eyes went wide. "Oh my gosh! Are you in love with her?"

Lucy stepped even closer, her eyes wide at the question, too.

Chris paused for a moment. "I mean, I love the time we spend together. I love how she makes me feel. I love the sex. And I miss her when we're apart. But is that"—Chris made quotes in the air with her fingers—"'in love'?"

Lucy shook her fists in the air and groaned through her teeth in frustration. "Yes, you dope! That's 'in love'!" she said, repeating the air quotes.

Chris shook her head, closing the back hatch of her car carefully so as not to crush any of the boxes inside. "No. It can't be. We only met a little over a month ago. We hardly know each other. And after what happened with you"—Chris gestured at Maddie—"how can I trust her?"

Maddie leaned in close to Chris. "We should compare notes. I mean, the orgasms with Angel were top-notch, but for me, emotionally…" Maddie made a so-so motion with her hand.

"Yeah, well, you're straight."

"When are we telling Mike?" asked Lucy.

Maddie nodded. "We should tell him as soon as possible. So he has time to be mad and get over it before the wedding."

Chris shook her head. "The wedding is less than a week away. You don't know if he'll be over it by then."

Lucy waved her hand. "He'll be over it and you'll be forgiven. Completely forgiven."

"Yeah, that's Mike," added Maddie. "He's like a dog that way. You could kick him across the room, and he'd still come back and lick your feet."

Lucy stuck out her tongue in disgust. "I do not need to hear about your sex kinks with my brother."

Maddie slapped Lucy on the shoulder good-naturedly. But as Lucy and Maddie laughed Chris stepped up to them, appalled.

"Oh, no, we can't tell him. Really, he can't know!"

Maddie put calming hands on Chris's shoulders. "It's a bad idea to keep this from him. It was a bad idea keeping it from us. You should have said something weeks ago."

Chris looked down at the ground. "I didn't want…I don't want Mike thinking badly of me."

Lucy scoffed. "So, he thinks you're a traitor and a skank for a while. Who gives a shit? I already sort of think that of you, but who the hell cares? You're still my friend."

Maddie looked at Lucy and whistled, "Wow, talk about the skank calling the skank skanky."

Lucy stuck out her chin. "Hey, I live my truth. And if we are talking skanky, I'm not the one who stepped out on my fiancé to try bumping donuts to see if I liked it."

Chris slapped her palm to her forehead. "God, why do I hang out with so many straight people?"

Maddie stepped up to her. "Tell him."

Lucy followed suit. "Tell him."

She thrust her hands out in a defensive position. "I'll tell him. I'll tell him. I just don't want him to know before the wedding. I'm supposed to be his best man. I don't want him thinking about what an untrustworthy disappointment I am when he is getting married."

Lucy and Maddie gave each other a look, then both looked at her. Lucy shook her head.

Maddie shrugged. "Your call, Chris."

Chris nodded. "We wait. We wait until after the wedding. Then I'll tell him that Angel and I are together."

* * *

Chris walked into Olivia's, which was still busy despite the fact it was a Monday night. She headed for the back room where Lucy and Maddie were getting ready for the rehearsal dinner. Mike was in a corner playing a game on his phone. He waved at Chris and she waved back. Chris walked over to Maddie and Lucy.

"Have you seen the cake yet?" asked Maddie.

"Go look at it. It's beautiful," said Lucy.

"Angel took it to the office to touch up a little bit of damage that happened during delivery. But it is beautiful," said Maddie.

"Okay. I can't wait to see it."

"Rehearsal starts in a half hour. Don't be late," said Maddie.

Lucy grinned at Chris. "Yeah. Don't get distracted."

Chris gave Lucy a sidelong look and turned and walked to the kitchen. She entered the kitchen and zigzagged her way past the busy staff toward the office.

"Hope the restaurant doesn't lose any more furniture," snarked Jo under her breath as Chris walked by. Jasper, standing next to Jo on the line, sniggered, and a couple of other staff stifled some giggles.

Chris rolled her eyes. Could she humiliate herself any more in front of these people? She made her way to the office, where Angel had the three-tier cake set up on the makeshift desk. With intense concentration she was piping some finishing touches on the elegant and perfectly symmetrical cake.

"Wow! Beautiful!" Chris said quietly so as not to startle Angel. Angel glanced up at her for a moment and smiled before returning her attention to the cake.

"Are you talking about me or the cake?"

"Both," said Chris. She stepped into the room and gently closed the door.

"Just needs a little repair. Nothing some piped frosting can't fix." Angel lowered her piping bag and stepped back to look the cake over.

"You can decorate cakes, too?"

"I told you. I'm a jack of all trades in the kitchen."

Angel put her hand on her nape and stretched her neck. "It's already been a busy day and the evening is just getting started."

Chris came up behind Angel and put her hands on her hips. "Wait until you open up the rooftop to the public and double your business. Then you'll really have some busy days."

Angel grinned and turned under Chris's hands to face her. Chris leaned in for a kiss, but Angel squeezed some frosting onto her finger and held it up to her mouth.

"Taste this. Tell me what you think."

Chris took Angel's hand in hers and directed the frosting-covered finger to her lips. She poked her tongue out and slowly dragged it across it. Angel's lips parted and she sucked in a quick breath. Chris took the frosting into her mouth and then closed her lips around the tip of the finger. With her tongue she began to tickle the fingertip suggestively.

Angel smiled at Chris and her eyelids lowered heavily. "I'm actually not on the schedule tonight. How about we go back to my place?"

"Rehearsal starts in a half hour."

"Maybe you could skip it?"

"I'm the best man."

"Too bad. Guess you are busy tonight."

Chris smiled and leaned in closer to Angel. "Well, I have a half hour right now."

Angel gave Chris a half smile and glanced at the cake on the desk. "Unfortunately, the desk is occupied."

Chris gave the waistband on Angel's slacks a downward tug and looked down at the floor before looking back up at Angel.

Angel grinned and slid a hand up Chris's side under her shirt. "Mmm. Floors don't hold too much appeal for me. How about after the rehearsal we go to my place, where we can climb into a nice, clean bed together."

Chris groaned. "Ugh! Why'd you have to give Mike a whole three hours for the rehearsal and dinner?"

"That's not a lot of time for a rehearsal and dinner. But I'll make sure my staff serves dinner fast and maybe we can get you out of here a little early."

"You're not going to stick around to help with cleanup?"

"I am not on the schedule so they can clean up without me."

Chris smiled, nodded, and kissed Angel's sweet, expectant lips.

* * *

Angel watched surreptitiously from a dark corner on the patio while an in-charge woman with a British accent, a crisp white blouse, and a gray, pencil-cut skirt directed Maddie and Mike, Chris and Lucy, and another woman, likely a musician or photographer, around Olivia's rooftop, telling them where to stand and which way to face.

"Okay! A quick run-through. Mike, take your place up front there. Chris, the groomswoman, you stand next to him on the right. Maddie, let's get your walk down the aisle timed with the music. The music's over there."

The Brit pointed to a corner, and the woman Angel didn't recognize, the musician, walked to that location.

Then the Brit took Maddie by the elbow and counted Maddie's steps as they walked to the back. She let go of Maddie and turned back to the musician. "You'll have how many with you?"

"Duet. Violin and classical guitar."

"Can you give us a nod as a signal before the last sixteen measures?"

The musician made a note.

"Okay, Maddie, watch the musician. When she nods, you walk like this. You'll hear it." And with her hand on Maddie's elbow the English woman started to hum Pachelbel's Canon in D, stepping with Maddie down the aisle toward Mike, under the pergola and against the west wall, taking a step at each measure. Then she stopped and walked Maddie backward toward the start again.

"Let's do that from the beginning."

The Brit suddenly stabbed her index finger in Angel's direction. "Who's that?"

Angel squirmed, having hoped she wouldn't be noticed in the corner. She looked up at Chris and Mike in the front and saw the eagerness in Chris's eyes upon noticing her while Mike flung daggers with his glare.

Maddie answered. "That's Angel Lux. She owns Olivia's."

"Hum it," she told Maddie. "You know the song." Then the woman pointed Maddie up the aisle. "Make your way to the front. Hold your bouquet."

Maddie snapped her hands up to hold her imaginary bouquet. Then she started humming and stepping her way to the front. Angel was going to slink back into the kitchen stairway when the woman turned on her heel and marched over to her with her right hand extended, her well-polished black leather pumps clapping the new decking loudly as she walked.

"I'm the officiant, Elizabeth Bentley of Elizabeth Bentley Weddings and Events."

Angel extended her right hand. The woman grasped and shook it firmly while at the same time handing Angel a business card with her other hand.

"Nice, romantic space you've made here," Bentley said, moving her eyes around the patio. "How many can you seat comfortably?"

"Fifty comfortably. Seventy-five if we squeeze. I'm just here to let everybody know we'll be serving dinner in the back room with the rest of the group in about fifteen min—"

"Back room. Could you use that as backup in bad weather? How many can fit in there?"

"I wouldn't go more than forty."

"Show me the far end there." Bentley pointed toward where Mike and Chris were standing. She gripped Angel's upper arm above the elbow and escorted Angel like a bailiff walking a reluctant defendant into court. She strode them past Maddie, who was still humming Pachelbel's Canon and stepping her way toward the front while holding her imaginary bouquet.

Bentley stopped with Angel in front of Mike and Chris. "I assume the dance floor—"

Bentley did a double take upon spotting Mike's glare at Angel, a glare that Angel had been all too aware of all evening. She turned to watch Angel. Angel tried to settle herself, shifting uncomfortably back and forth under the stare, like a frightened rabbit who could dart away at the slightest threat. Then Angel narrowed her eyes at Mike and lifted her chin. She would never give him that satisfaction!

Bentley nodded to herself slightly.

Just when Angel thought Bentley was going to inquire about the obvious hostility in the room, Bentley did a second double take, this time at Chris, who was making no attempt to conceal her dreamy eyes as she gazed at Angel. Nor was Chris doing a very good job at concealing the way she was rubbing her inner thighs together in a peculiar manner.

Angel grinned, knowing the reason for the fidgeting. Bentley snapped an accusatory look at Angel. *Crap!* Apparently, Angel wasn't the only one who had figured out that Chris was coping with an uncomfortable lady-boner and that Angel, herself, was the cause.

Bentley slowly turned to look at Mike again. "I see." She paused briefly and then turned back to Angel. "So, the tables will be back there, and this area will be set up with chairs for the ceremony?"

"Yes," said Angel. "While the congregants are served dinner, the chairs will be removed from this area and it will be converted to the dance floor. A deejay will set up over there." She pointed to one corner of the patio.

Bentley looked up at the clear evening sky as the sun started to descend. "I checked the weather, and it looks like we can count on clear skies on Saturday, though that is still five days away. Let's hope that forecast holds up."

Maddie arrived at the front with the rest of the group.

"Oh, good. You made it Maddie!" said Bentley brightly. "Stand right here." Then Bentley barked, "Maid of honor!"

Lucy jumped up and ran to stand next to Maddie.

Bentley nodded and took her position in front of the couple. "I'll be standing here. I'll say a few lovely words. There will be a little laughter, a few tears. You'll say your vows. Have you written them?"

Maddie nodded, and Mike pulled a piece of paper out of his pocket and started to read the text scrawled upon it. "Madelyn—"

Bentley turned to Mike. "Not now, dear. We'll save it for the wedding." Bentley returned to speaking to the group. "Then there will be an exchange of rings. Maid of honor, you'll give the ring to Madelyn, and she'll put it on Michael's left-hand ring finger. Hold up your left hand, Mr. Lundgren."

Mike held up his right hand. Then he put it down and held up his left.

Bentley continued, gesturing to Chris. "Then the groomswoman will give the ring to Mike, and he will put the ring on Maddie's left-hand ring finger. Hold up your left hand, Madelyn."

Maddie held up her left hand and then put it down. Mike followed, putting his hand down as well.

"Then there is a kiss for the bride. I will signal the musicians like this." Bentley pointed at the musician, who nodded. "Walking back is easier. Mike and Maddie go first, followed by the maid of honor and the groomswoman. Take your time. Don't run. People will want to take pictures as you go back down the aisle. Your first steps together as a married couple. And you four just go to the head table which will be set up…"

Bentley pointed at Angel.

"Right there," she said, pointing at a spot on the patio.

"Right there," said Bentley, pointing to the spot for Mike and Maddie. Bentley clapped her hands together. "And that's all there is to it. The rehearsal dinner will be served downstairs in the back room in five minutes."

CHAPTER EIGHTEEN

Angel, with intense focus, lightly dusted confectioners' sugar onto the tops of row after row of individual white ramekins filled with black cherry clafouti while the kitchen buzzed in chaos around her. A couple of staff members slammed into the kitchen carrying enormous trays of empty plates.

Angel never looked away from her ramekins. "Is the main course completely cleared?"

"Yes, Chef," declared both staff, dumping the dirty dishes into the dish pit.

"Good." She stepped away from the counter, removed the dish towel perpetually thrown over her shoulder, and leaned back in to tidy up the sides of several ramekins. She turned to grab some trays to help get them served. "Then let's get dessert served and get this fucking rehearsal dinner over wi—Jesus Christ!" Angel exclaimed, spinning into the enormous Mike blocking her way. "What the *fuck* are you doing in my kitchen! And how the *hell* does an ox like you sneak up on somebody like that? Get out of here!"

"Were you looking at Maddie? I saw you looking at Maddie!"

Angel's face went red in anger, and she took a step toward Mike. "Yeah. I'm short on servers so I may have glanced at your girlfriend so I didn't fucking drop her plate in her lap!"

Mike, his face reddening as well, took a step toward her. "Well, I didn't like the *way* you looked at—!"

"I didn't look at her any goddamn way, you bonehead! You're just—"

"What did you call me? A bonehead?" Mike took another intimidating step toward Angel.

Unable to get closer without making contact, Angel cranked her head back to look at Mike as directly in the eye as she could, given the way he towered over her. "Yeah. A bonehead! A big, ugly ogre with a thick, giant *bonehead*!" she yelled, her eyes flaring.

"You're calling me names and you're the one lookin' at my fiancé, the woman I am going to marry in five days—"

"Gentlepeople, please!" Bentley wedged herself between Mike and Angel, shoving Mike back a good foot with her hands and knocking Angel back a step with her hip. Chris was right behind her, putting her shoulder into Mike and knocking him back another couple of feet. She braced her shoulder against him and planted her feet in the ground to keep him back. Then Bentley, facing Mike, but clearly talking to both him and Angel, quietly, but very firmly said, "All of your friends and family can hear you in the back room."

Mike's angry expression turned sheepish. Chris kept her shoulder against him.

Angel crossed her arms over her chest in a sulk. "Not my family."

Bentley looked over her shoulder at Angel. "Then how about your customers, dear? Do you want to read about a screaming match in Olivia's kitchen in a Yelp review tomorrow?"

Now it was Angel's turn to look sheepish.

Firmness turned to anger, and Bentley stabbed a finger toward the back room. "Maddie is practically in tears hearing you two screaming at each other."

Mike looked at Chris. She nodded to confirm the information.

Angel and Mike bowed their heads in unison, looking at the same piece of floor under Bentley's shiny black pumps. Chris took her shoulder out of Mike's chest and stepped back.

Bentley continued. "Should that kind, lovely woman in there be crying at the rehearsal dinner for her wedding or should she be happy?"

Well scolded, Angel and Mike mumbled, "Happy."

Bentley looked at the staff, who had all stopped working to stare at the scene. She turned to Angel. "Those clafouti won't serve themselves."

Angel circled her hand over her head to signal action. "Get back to work!" she barked. The staff jumped, grabbing trays of ramekins and rushing out of the kitchen.

Bentley turned to Chris. "Tell Maddie everything is okay."

She nodded. She looked over at Mike, who seemed adequately subdued, then turned back to glance at Angel. Angel did a quick nod to Chris, indicating that everything was okay and Chris left.

Bentley turned back to Mike and Angel. "You two hate each other. Fine! But you're going to go in there and be civil to each other tonight and through Maddie's wedding day on Saturday, all day Saturday, because you're adults and you can make it one day and the rest of tonight without getting into a fight not fit for elementary school children on a playground!"

Mike snuck one last glare at Angel, then dropped his expression back to contrition. He nodded at Bentley as she turned to him. Angel returned the glare while Bentley was looking at him but dropped it quickly when Bentley turned to watch Angel's acknowledgment. She nodded.

"Mr. Lundgren, go in there, sit down, and apologize to Maddie and tell her it won't happen again."

Mike nodded and left for the dining room.

"Ms. Lux, I believe this is the last tray of ramekins that needs to be served." Bentley pointed at the tray on the table that Angel had been working on.

Angel stiffened at being bossed around her own kitchen but nodded. She picked up the large tray of ramekins and exited the kitchen.

Angel held an empty tray while Jo piled it high with cleaned out ramekins from the head table. Jo reached down and picked up the empty dish in front of Mike as he delicately tapped at the corners of his mouth with his cloth napkin.

"Thank you, Chef. That custard cherry thing was delicious."

Angel wanted to smash the tray of empty ramekins over his fat head, but she glanced at Chris and Maddie and the Brit, who were all watching her carefully. Instead, she smiled at Mike brightly.

"I'm glad you enjoyed it."

"What's it called?"

"Black cherry clafouti."

Mike screwed up his face at the foreign word. "Clah… flau… Well, it's good anyway. You should put it on your regular menu."

Angel shuddered a bit at receiving menu advice from this lummox. But she gave him a big, cheerful smile instead. "Thanks for the suggestion, Mike. Maybe I'll do that."

"That and shrimp. You don't have any shellfish on your menu. What's up with that?"

Jo set the last of the empty ramekins on the tray, and Angel whisked them off to the kitchen.

In the kitchen, she threw the ramekins in the dish pit while the other staff buzzed around her. She grabbed the chef's cap off her head and cursed the evening under her breath. Fortunately, the dinner would be over soon. Then she would take Chris back to her apartment and take her to bed.

Angel leaned against the wall and closed her eyes for a quick breather. First, before they got into bed, she would undress Chris. She'd unbutton her shirt and remove the fabric of the shirt from one tanned shoulder and then from the other. She'd let the shirt fall to the floor. Then she would step closer and reach around to undo the clasp on her bra. She'd pull the straps off her shoulders and down her muscular arms and drop the bra next to the shirt. She'd run her hands down her smooth shoulders, over her firm breasts and down her flat stomach till she got to the waistband of her pants. There she'd undo the button and the zipper. She'd unfasten them slowly. She'd make a point of not being in a rush tonight. Slow moves seemed to make Chris go wild.

Then she'd put her hands on her small waist and turn her around so her round, generous bottom was in front of her. She would hook the waistband of Chris's pants and her panties with her thumbs and tug them both down over her womanly hips until those fell on the floor, too. She'd let Chris step out of them, and then, as Angel admired her well-muscled back as it tapered down to her narrow waist and then flared out again into that glorious ass, she would whisper her name, "Chris."

And Chris would whisper back, "Angel."

Angel took a deep breath as she listened to the racket in the kitchen as the last of the night's dishes were cleared. She imagined Chris's voice again. "Angel."

"Hey! Psst! Angel!"

Angel's eyes snapped open when she realized the words weren't in her imagination anymore. She peered in the direction of the voice and turned to see Chris crouched in the doorway to the kitchen, trying not to be noticed by the staff. Angel stuffed her tie-back cap in her pocket and pointed toward the stairway. They slid past the staff and hurried up the kitchen stairs to the rooftop.

Once on the dark rooftop, lit only by the emergency lighting over the doors, they headed over to the pergola. Chris got there first. She turned to face Angel, took her face in her hands, and kissed her deeply. Angel kissed her back with equal passion.

Chris moved her hands down to Angel's waist and her mouth to her ear and gently took Angel's earlobe in her mouth and kissed it. Angel shuddered. She pushed her hands under Chris's shirt and ran them up her smooth, warm back.

"Can you leave the rest of the night to your crew so we can go to your place now?" Chris breathed into Angel's neck.

Angel nodded and grabbed her hand. "Come on, let's go."

Angel slammed into Mike, who was standing in the middle of the dark rooftop, and then slammed into him again as Chris collided with her from behind. They bounced off him like they had run into a wall. Mike strode closer to them, backing Chris and Angel up several feet.

"What is wrong with you!" he bellowed at Angel. "I came back to the kitchen to settle my bill with you and they said to look for you up here and I find this!"

"This isn't your business!" Angel yelled back at him.

Mike started arguing. It was Angel's intention to argue back, but Chris had her wrist firmly grasped in her hand and was dragging her across the patio to the customer stairway.

"Chris is my best friend! And my best man!" Mike howled down the stairway. Angel desperately tried to keep her feet under her while trying to turn and yell back at Mike as the deceptively strong Chris towed her down the stairs toward the building entrance.

"And you've got your hands all over her at my rehearsal dinner!" Mike's voice echoed off the walls of the stairway, and he bounded down the stairs after them.

At almost the bottom of the stairway Angel was able to wrap her free hand around the banister and managed to stop Chris from dragging her any farther. She spun her head over her shoulder toward Mike, whose large frame filled the small stairway. "So what! Your fiancée is in there. Chris isn't tied to anybody. She broke up with David so she can date anybody she wants now, including me!"

Chris wrapped her other hand around Angel's forearm and gave her a hard yank, forcing her to let go of the banister and stumble down the last couple stairs to the restaurant entryway, where Chris grabbed her to keep her from falling on the floor.

Angel leaned over Chris's arm to continue her tirade. "Even if she was still engaged, she has the right to be with whomever she wants, and that includes me!"

"David?" Mike's face screwed up in confusion as he pounded down the last few stairs.

Mike landed at the entrance with them, and Chris put a hand up to stop him. "Mike—"

Crowded out of the small entrance with Mike's arrival, Angel pushed the restaurant door open with her back. Suddenly all three of them were standing in the middle of the pedestrian promenade of State Street.

Angel took a step toward Mike and Chris grabbed her wrist again, but Angel yanked it away and pushed past her to stand toe-to-toe with Mike. "Yeah. That's right. Chris dumped David. They aren't getting married. And if you were *really* her best friend, you would have known that!"

Mike stood for a moment, his brow puckered in confusion, but then his face started to open with realization.

Bentley pushed open the restaurant door and headed toward them.

Chris stepped up between Mike and Angel, wedging the two apart. "Mike, stop. Angel, listen—"

"Ooooh," brayed Mike over Chris's head to Angel. "Is that what she told you?"

Chris had both hands up to Mike now. "Mike, don't—"

"That she was dating some guy named David?" Mike howled in laughter.

Chris turned to face Angel. Angel, utterly confused, stared back at her.

"That was just part of the trap! That was our plan, to have *Chris* seduce *you!*" Mike pointed a fat finger at Angel.

Then Maddie was at Mike's left shoulder and Lucy was at his right side. Angel didn't know when they had gotten there.

"Mike, come back to the dining room," said Maddie calmly, but Mike just jammed his finger repeatedly at Angel.

"Chris got you away from Maddie so I could get Maddie back!"

Confused, Angel turned her back on Mike and took a step toward Chris. "What is he saying about David?"

The pain and sadness in Chris's face really confused Angel.

Chris put her hands on her shoulders. "Angel, let me explain."

"There is no David!" Mike yelled at Angel at the volume of a jet engine. Angel turned her head to look at him. "Chris has been gay since she kissed a girl in middle school! She's never even had sex with a man!"

Angel turned to Chris, waiting for her to explain David to this big, dumb fool. But when she saw tears of frustration start to roll down her face, it began to be apparent who the real big, dumb fool was.

"Chris…" Angel croaked.

Chris stormed over to confront Mike. "Shut up, Mike!"

Mike ignored her and stepped past her to confront Angel again. "The plan was to string you along until the wedding and then she was going to dump you!" He looked over his shoulder at Chris. "Right, Chris? That's what you told me last Saturday. You were dumping her after the wedding." He pointed at Angel again. "Tell her!"

Chris drove forward and shoved Mike out of the way. She grabbed Angel's shoulders again as tears started to spill out of Angel's eyes as well. "I can explain."

Angel choked a couple of times and rubbed the scar on her brow in frustration. She finally managed to get out her question. "Does David exist?"

Chris paused, tears streaming down her face. Gathering herself together, she said, "There's no David. But it doesn't matter."

Angel had heard enough. She felt her face go beet red with humiliation, suddenly aware of the crowd that had gathered around them: Jasper and Jo, Maddie and Lucy, some other staff and people from the party, and a whole crowd of college kids who had started hooting and chanting at their fight.

All she knew at this point was that she had to get away.

Chris grabbed her arm. "Angel!"

"Let go of me!" She tore her arm away. "Leave me alone!" Tears streaming down her face, she spun away from Chris and the restaurant and toward the end of the street where Bentley was standing.

Mike howled in laughter and yelled at Angel's retreating frame. "That's right! The seductress trap worked! You've been scammed, Angel Lux! Fooled! Chris made a fool of you!"

Bentley caught Angel's shoulders before she could break into a flat run down the street and spoke directly to her. "If you think that woman doesn't love you, there has been a grave misunderstanding."

As Mike's laughter echoed down the street, Angel tore herself from Bentley's grasp and raced away.

CHAPTER NINETEEN

Angel looked at herself in the bar-length mirror behind the bottles of alcohol. She moved her hand to slick back a loose curl behind her ear. She shook her empty glass at the bartender with the blue beehive and set it on the bar. She glanced at herself again in the mirror and straightened the collar on her denim jacket as the bartender refilled her drink.

The night before she had blocked Chris's cell number and spent the evening crying her eyes out like a heartbroken teenager, but if there was one thing Angel knew she could do it was to get back up on her feet after a blow that would leave somebody else down for the count.

She brought the wet, cold glass to her mouth and turned to see the action on the stage. A well-muscled man in a G-string humped the stripper pole while a gaggle of women and gay men screamed at his feet.

The bartender wiped down the bar in front of Angel. She leaned in conspiratorially and Angel turned to her.

"Looks like you have an admirer." The bartender bobbed her blue beehive to the left.

Angel gave a quick nod in acknowledgment, putting an extra bill down for a tip. She smiled. The denim jacket always got a nibble.

She took a sip of her drink and, slowly turning her head in the direction indicated by the blue beehive, she saw a very pretty young woman in a little, black dress watching her carefully from the end of the bar.

Embarrassed at having been caught staring at Angel, the woman looked down at the floor and then off toward the stage, but after a few moments her gaze returned to Angel and from across the bar she looked directly and boldly into her eyes.

Angel licked her thumb and slicked down the wild tuft on her eyebrow. She put another couple of bills on the bar to pay off her tab, then she picked up her coaster and drink, and took a couple of steps toward the woman in the little, black dress. She stiffened in excitement and anticipation and then turned to look down the other end of the bar, trying to appear nonchalant about Angel's approach.

Angel quickly formulated her game plan. The young woman apparently had had a couple of drinks already, but she still looked quite alert, so there would be no need to wait for her to sober up. She was probably here with her straight girlfriends but had managed to slip away so she could check out Angel without them watching. Angel knew she would have to charm the friends so when this woman announced to them a change in plans—a headache but her new friend Angel would take her home or a sudden, desperate need for a coffee away from here but with Angel—they would not object. Once Angel had the woman separated from her friends it would be a cinch to get the woman back to her apartment.

Angel realized suddenly that she wasn't moving. She looked down at her feet, confused as to why they were planted on the floor and preventing her from making any progress toward her target.

The young woman looked up at Angel from heavy lashes, which she batted a couple of times in her direction. She couldn't have made her intentions clearer if she had held a sign over her head that read, "Please hit on me."

Angel's feet still weren't moving. The too-loud beat from the dance floor was making her head throb, and the flashing stage lights were annoying as hell. The smell of stale beer and sweat was disgusting, and the woman at the end of the bar, though pretty, would probably be in her bed for just one night. The chances that they would do any talking at all, or if they did talk, that the talk would be interesting, were next to zilch. She had come to the club looking for straight girls and a little fun, but it was suddenly clear to Angel that this place held no enjoyment for her anymore.

Angel decided to take the cue from her uncooperative feet. She politely smiled and nodded to the young woman, set her almost full drink on the bar, turned, and left the building.

* * *

The corner of the shop held a dog bed and on top of it a very tired puppy, in the middle of a huge yawn. Chris had picked her up at the pound only the day before, and they were still getting to know each other. The puppy's pedigree was a complete mystery. "Large and hairy" was about all that could be promised regarding her adulthood; the staff at the shelter had been calling her "Bear" because of her enormous paws. But she was friendly and healthy, eager to please, and too dopey to be afraid of anything. All perfect personality traits to guarantee a great dog in the future.

Chris figured she'd need a new friend now, anyway. After the rehearsal dinner, when Angel had run away from Olivia's, Maddie had slugged Mike hard in the shoulder. He ignored Maddie and lifted his palm in the air and held it out for Chris.

"High-five, best man! That was so perfect!"

Chris had turned to face Mike, tears streaming down her face, and in front of the crowd of strangers on the street she had yelled at him, "Find another best man! And another best friend!" before she had stormed off, clapping her hands over her ears to shut out the calls from her friends.

She had lost her dearest friend and likely her business, too. She looked around the shop. This was probably not a great time to get a dog. She had no idea what would happen to this place now.

She looked down at Bear. The pup's tongue was lolling out of her head as she dozed away in the dog bed. Chris had spent the whole day trying to run the energy out of her, but the pup's enthusiasm for play seemed, for a time, like it might be boundless. It was the least she could do after she took Bear home and cried into her new puppy's furry face all night. Now that afternoon was moving to evening, though, the puppy was finally tuckered out.

Chris went to check on the piece she had built with the slab. She double checked the stability of the legs and the gaps on all the joins. The finish had turned out perfectly and looked like crystal-clear glass on top of the slab. She checked it under the light from several directions, searching for a single flaw, a speck of dust under the finish, a tiny scratch, or a single mark from a single hair of a single brushstroke, but she couldn't find any.

"Hey, you," said Lucy from the doorway, letting herself into the shop.

Chris glanced back at Lucy briefly before returning her attention to the slab. "Hey."

"I've been trying to reach you, but you haven't returned any of my calls."

Chris put her index finger to her lips, indicating "Quiet," and then gestured to the sleeping puppy in the bed.

"A puppy! Aw!" Lucy started to rush over to Bear, but Chris stopped her.

"No. She's finally just asleep."

Lucy turned back to Chris.

Chris pointed to some boxes in the corner. "Those are the decorations. I'll help you get them in your car."

She reached in her pocket and pulled out two gold wedding bands. She walked them over to Lucy and held them out to her. Lucy did not reach out to take them.

"He still wants you as his best man tomorrow. He regrets very much what he said. He wants you to know he is very, very sorry."

Chris dropped the hand with the rings to her side. Her eyes started to well up. "He's sorry, but it's all my fault. And now Angel…"

Chris couldn't finish. Her throat choked up, and she let out a big sob. Lucy wrapped her arms around her, and she planted her face in Lucy's shoulder and bawled.

* * *

Angel, in a fluffy, white bathrobe, her short hair wet from the shower, sat on her overstuffed sofa with a cup of coffee in her hand. The morning summer sun streamed in through the open window and billowed the sheer drapes gently. Curling her bare legs underneath her, she leaned over to set the coffee on the end table. She glanced at the happy picture of herself and Olivia there, both grinning with their arms around each other. She reached over and picked it up. She held the picture and stroked a thumb over Olivia's face, following her cheek.

A smile tugged at the corner of Angel's mouth at the beautiful grin on Olivia's face and then a tear fell from her eye. She impatiently brushed it away, but then another came, and another, and another. Wracking sobs followed; she missed Olivia so very much. Through the pain, she realized that she wasn't as usual crying angry tears over having lost her wife, but ones born of deep sadness. That lack of anger was something completely new for her.

* * *

Sunlight blinked through the curtains and Bear busied herself with a game of tug of war with the blankets on the bed while Chris tried to sleep.

"Bear."

The tug-of-war game pulled the blanket off her.

"Bear! It's too early."

Bear let out a little yelp at her.

Chris sat up. "House-training," she groggily reminded herself. "House-training the puppy." She turned to the pup. "Who's got to go potty?"

Bear yipped again.

"Okay. Let's go out. Let's go out quick!"

Bear yipped some more as she threw on a robe and stepped into her slippers. She grabbed her phone and her keys and headed for her apartment door. Bear's leash hung next to the door. She snapped it on the puppy's collar, and they left the apartment.

Once outside, Chris, in her pajamas and bathrobe, walked the puppy back and forth in the grass on the boulevard of the residential street, offering words of grand encouragement for Bear. Bear, still unfamiliar with the concept of a leash, repeatedly choked herself as she tried to chase after every bug and leaf that crossed her path.

Chris's phone rang. She pulled it out of her robe pocket and checked the caller ID. It was Lucy. She answered it.

"Chris! I need your help!"

"What's going on?"

"I'm at the hospital with Jasper."

"Jasper? From Olivia's?"

"He told me he was allergic to shellfish. I didn't feed him any, but I had a snack from my fridge this morning. Turns out he is *really* allergic to shellfish. Did you know that if somebody is really allergic to a certain food you must not kiss them after you've been eating that certain food? You cannot kiss them. Don't do it."

"What? Why are you kissing Jasper?"

"I was supposed to help decorate the patio this morning for the wedding at sunset, but I can't make it. Can you do it for me?"

"Lucy...I don't...I can't...I have this puppy now—"

"Please, Chris. Don't worry about Mike. He's not coming to the restaurant till the last minute. And Angel already told Jasper that she wouldn't be there today. Do it for Maddie."

Chris sighed.

"Maddie is so upset about everything. She blames herself for the rift between you and Mike and for you losing Angel."

"It wasn't her fault."

"She doesn't feel that way. She thinks you hate her."

"I don't hate her."

"Please?" Lucy added. "Do it for me, too? Friend?"

Chris sighed in defeat while the puppy pottied on the grass.

"Could you have Jasper send Jo to the shop? There's something I need her to help me with."

"Sure. We'll do that."

Chris hung up the phone, picked up the puppy, and praised her for pottying on the grass. She got lots of puppy kisses back.

She put Bear back down on the ground. "You haven't been crate trained yet. I can't put you in there for hours your first time. What am I going to do with you?"

Bear cocked her fluffy head at Chris.

* * *

Bear tugged on one end of a string of white, fairy lights as Jo tugged on the other side.

"Bear! Let go. Come on!"

Jo reached down, picked up the puppy, and worked on getting the lights out of her mouth. When she finally got the lights away from her, Jo was rewarded for her efforts with big, slobbery puppy kisses all over her face.

"Eech! Bear!"

Chris climbed off the ladder, having finished hanging sheer white drapes overhead on the pergola. They created the illusion of a ceiling but were still spaced apart enough to allow glimpses of the sky and eventual starlight above. She took the string of lights from Jo while Jo cuddled the puppy and climbed back up the ladder to start hanging those. The tables were already dressed with white tablecloths and linen napkins, white plates, and sparkling silverware. She and Jo had installed a fresh flower shroud around the pergola that would frame the couple and officiant for the main part of the ceremony. The chairs were set up for attendees to watch the ceremony. The last job would be to put fresh flowers in the centerpieces, which were already on the tables. In a couple of hours they would be done.

"Should we go to the car and get the…?" Jo asked at the bottom of the ladder, holding the puppy.

Chris nodded and descended the ladder.

* * *

Chris and Jo were finishing up the twinkle lights, checking the connections, and looking for any burnt-out bulbs when Lucy arrived with more fresh flowers.

Chris folded up the ladder and put it to the side. Lucy came up to her and they hugged.

"How is Jasper?" asked Chris.

"He's better. The swelling is coming down. Christ, his head was so swollen he looked like a human bobblehead, but he'll be fine."

Wordlessly, Chris, Jo, and Lucy finished the centerpieces, each taking turns entertaining Bear until the pup finally collapsed in a shady spot and fell asleep. Bentley arrived just as the rooftop was finished and announced she was there to check on the progress. The three held their breath waiting for her reaction as she narrowed her eyes and walked through the space, checking each table, each place setting, and each individual piece of silverware.

"I thought this woman was just the officiant," Jo whispered to Chris and Lucy.

"She is. She's not in charge of any of this. She was just hired to do the ceremony," Lucy whispered back.

Bentley picked up a wineglass from one of the tables and inspected it in the morning sunlight. She turned to the women and held the glass in the air.

"Spots!" Bentley barked.

Jo ran to grab the glass. When she got to Bentley, she held out her hand for the glass. Bentley extended the glass to her but didn't hand it over yet.

"How is staffing tonight?"

"Jasper is out sick, and Angel isn't coming in, so we'll be a little shorthanded."

"You're expecting the usual dinner crowd in the main restaurant tonight, plus you'll be serving the wedding party out here?"

"Yes."

"So you'll be a lot shorthanded," said Bentley, handing the glass to Jo.

"Yes."

Jo took the glass and ran to the kitchen stairway with it while Chris and Lucy gathered up boxes and packing to take to the Subaru. As Chris loaded the empty boxes Lucy went back to the patio. Returning with the sleeping puppy, she put her in a crate sitting on the back seat. Chris moved around the car and opened the driver's door.

Lucy put a hand on her arm. "Please come back for the wedding. Please. You don't have to be the best man but stay for the wedding. We'll all feel terrible if you aren't there. Please, Chris. I feel so horrible about everything that has happened."

Chris sighed. "I'm sorry. I love you all, but—"

Chris watched tears well up in Lucy's eyes and her bottom lip start to tremble.

"No." Chris shook her head. "You can't. Don't. Don't cry! I can't stand it when women cry!"

A big tear topped over Lucy's bottom lid and rolled dramatically down her cheek. "Please."

Chris sighed deeply in defeat.

* * *

Angel jumped as her phone rang in the pocket of her bathrobe. Groggily, she lifted her head. She had exhausted herself with the very hard cry. The tears had stopped some time ago, but her throat hurt, her face felt puffy, and her vision was blurred.

She attempted a sip from her coffee cup on the nearby end table while her phone continued to ring, but it was stone cold. Clearing her throat, she pulled her phone out of her pocket. She tried to make out the text on the screen to identify the caller, but it was too blurry to read. She decided to answer it.

"Hello?"

"Angel Lux? This is Elizabeth Bentley."

"Bentley Weddings and Events. Yeah?"

"Jasper is out of commission and the restaurant will be shorthanded tonight. They'll need you."

Angel was speechless for a moment. She had given her word that Mike and Maddie could use the rooftop for their wedding, but she had made it clear there was no way she would be coming into the restaurant today.

She groaned.

Bentley kept going. "Your head chef is out. Jo can try to cover for him, but she's not ready to do it herself yet, and she'll need your help. Your staff can handle the service on the floor. I promise, none of the wedding party will be allowed back in the kitchen."

"I don't think—"

"It will be the inaugural moment for your event space. People will talk. Mike and Maddie have a lot of friends in this town and a lot of them will be at Olivia's tonight. Trust me, you don't want this to go poorly."

Angel collapsed back on the couch, her palm over her face, and sighed deeply in defeat.

CHAPTER TWENTY

"Table three was supposed to be sauce served on the side. Re-fire now!" Angel, in her chef's coat and tie-back, yelled at her crew in the steamy kitchen while she focused on the final touches on the plate in front of her.

"Yes, Chef!" somebody yelled back.

Angel finished the plate and put it up on the pass, swiping a sleeve across the sweat beading up on her forehead with one arm while beginning to plate another dish with the other.

Jo ran up to Angel. "Can the bride use the office to get ready for the wedding?"

Angel glanced up at Lucy and Maddie in the kitchen doorway. She briefly nodded at Jo, who hurried back to the women and escorted them to the office.

"I need another side of béarnaise, on the fly!"

"Yes, Chef!"

Angel walked over to a bubbling pot while the cook stepped aside. Angel dipped a clean spoon in and carefully tasted the brew. She nodded her approval and discarded the spoon while the cook moved the pot off the stove.

Jo appeared at Angel's elbow again. "Chef?"

Angel glanced at Jo, who nodded toward the doorway. Angel looked up and saw Mike, in his tux, standing in the doorway looking at her. "Tell him to go away."

"I did. He won't. He says he needs to talk to you."

Angel glared at Mike and strode over to him. His face brightened.

"I said you could have the rooftop and we would cook the meal. I keep my word. But I do not—"

"I need to apologize to you."

"No. I don't give a fuck—"

"Please? Please, man, please. Maddie is mad at me. Lucy is mad at me. Chris isn't even speaking to me, and she was supposed to be my best man at the wedding. I really need to apologize to you."

A staff person tried to squeeze past the enormous man and, exasperated, Angel pushed him out of the kitchen and led him to the hallway by the bathrooms for a modicum of privacy.

Angel crossed her arms over her chest and looked skeptically up at Mike. "What?"

"It's true that we came up with this lame plan to get you away from Maddie. Maddie and I have since talked, and I understand now that Maddie is responsible for her own decisions. She's the one who made a commitment to me. Not you. And she's the one responsible for her own broken promises. Again, not you. But at the time, getting you away from Maddie seemed like the thing to do. Lucy and I came up with the plan. Chris didn't want to go along with it."

Angel scoffed. "But she did."

"She did. And that's how it started. But..." Mike rolled his eyes before gathering himself back together. "Lucy and Maddie say Chris is in love with you."

Angel's breath caught in her throat.

"They say she's really in love with you. I believe it. And I really hurt her when I said those things to you after the rehearsal dinner. Chris is my best friend and I hurt her badly." Tears started to well up. "And I hurt you. I hurt you both. And I regret it. And for that I am very, very sorry." Big tears started to roll down his cheeks. "Please forgive me."

Mike wiped his face on his tux sleeve, but Angel didn't really hear much after Mike said the part about Chris being in love with her.

"Please forgive Chris."

That Angel heard.

"Look." Mike folded his hands together in front of him as if in prayer. "Maddie and I went through a tough spot there with you and everything and I forgave her, and I feel so much better about that. I was so mad about what happened and at you, but it doesn't matter to me anymore." Tears continued to roll down his face. "Now I'm so happy!" he sobbed.

Angel took a step to get around Mike to walk away, but he stopped her with a hand on her arm. "Don't let anger ruin something special. The anger is never worth it."

Lucy appeared from behind Mike's enormous frame. "Mike, you should head to the rooftop." She looked at his wet face, grabbed a handkerchief from her purse, and started mopping up the tears and snot. "Ugh! I knew you'd cry. We'll be starting in an hour."

Mike took Lucy's handkerchief and then took his own handkerchief out of his pocket to finish up on his face. "Is Chris here yet?"

Lucy glanced at Angel before looking back to Mike. She shook her head. Mike bawled into the two handkerchiefs, and he turned around and headed for the stairway. Lucy started to follow him like she wanted to help but then threw up her hands in defeat.

Lucy turned to face Angel. "I blame—"

A tear rolled out of Angel's eye and down her cheek. She quickly swiped it away. "Just say it."

Lucy sighed. She put a comforting hand on Angel's arm and squeezed. "It doesn't matter anymore." And then she turned and headed for the office.

Angel stood in the hallway by the bathrooms for a moment. She leaned heavily against the wall, wiped her eyes, and attempted to gather herself together. She was taking a step toward the kitchen when Chris suddenly burst through the back entrance.

She froze upon spotting Angel. Angel froze too. They looked at each other for a moment, neither saying anything. When they did speak, it was both at the same time and they said the same thing. "I thought you weren't coming."

Chris was in a pretty floral summer dress, her honey-blond locks spilling over her shoulders as she teetered a bit on the heels. Angel flashed back to seeing Chris in the restaurant in the tight, sexy red dress, with nothing on underneath, remembering that it all was just part of a plan to trap her. She shook her head at her own gullibility.

Elizabeth Bentley suddenly strode out of the ladies' room and bumped into them both.

Surprise filled her face. "Oh!"

The spell that Angel had been under broke, and she started to head for the kitchen.

"Angel…" Chris extended a hand toward her, but she turned away and hurried back to the kitchen.

* * *

Chris lingered in a corner of the rooftop, trying to remain unnoticed in the crowd. A couple of people complimented her on the construction of the patio. She nodded but was in no mood for compliments and chitchat. She watched as Lucy opened a wheelchair next to the door for the main stairway and locked the wheels. Then Mike appeared through the door, in his tux, carrying his grandmother in his arms like she was a small child. He carefully set her in the chair and fussed with her legs to make sure they were set comfortably in the footrests.

She turned to look at the door to the kitchen stairway, as she had been doing since she got to the rooftop, hoping for the barest glimpse of Angel.

"Tell me something." Bentley had stepped up beside her. "You're a contractor, right?"

Chris nodded.

"So, hypothetically speaking, not me, of course, but if somebody made a really big mistake, like, put their car in drive instead of reverse and drove their car through their attached garage wall and right into the kitchen. They stupidly, negligently took a wall right out of their house. What's a person to do? I mean, what steps would you take, as a contractor, if that happened to you? I'm asking for a friend."

"Well, I'd inspect the damage, salvage what I could, demolish the rest, get materials, and I'd fix it."

"What if there is serious structural damage?"

Chris shrugged. "It will probably be more work and more money, but even structural damage can be repaired."

"That's what you do, isn't it? You fix things."

Chris nodded.

Bentley looked toward the kitchen stairway and then bobbed her head in that direction. "So, stop standing in the big disaster you made with your thumb up your arse and go fix it."

* * *

Angel took a step back from the line during a momentary lull. She took a deep breath and checked the time on a nearby clock. The ceremony would be starting soon. Then the kitchen would have an hour to start serving the wedding party. First, though, she and Jo were going to have to carry the wedding cake from the walk-in, up the stairway, to the rooftop. All the while the main dining room would be filling up with the regular dinner patrons. It was going to be crazy.

Jo stepped up to Angel like she had been reading Angel's mind.

"Get ready to get the cake upstairs," Angel told her.

"Maddie wants to talk to you in the office."

Angel glanced at the clock again and then nodded.

She stepped into the office just as Lucy was helping Maddie stand up from the chair. Angel smiled at the sight of the beautiful, petite brunette in a shimmering, satin, white gown. There was not a hint of lace anywhere; lace apparently was not Maddie's style. It completely suited her.

Maddie held her arms out for a hug and Angel happily obliged.

"I would have always wondered, you know?" Maddie looked at Angel with her big brown eyes. "Thank you for helping me figure that out."

Angel nodded. "Be happy."

Maddie placed a hand on Angel's cheek and looked at her with a sudden fierce intensity. "You, too."

Lucy stepped up to them. "Come on, Maddie. We should get set." Then Lucy took Maddie's hands in hers and smiled. "You're getting married."

Maddie grinned and said, in complete wonderment, "I'm getting married!"

Lucy started to walk Maddie out of the room. Angel stepped to the side as Lucy passed by. Just before they left the office, she turned to Angel and said, "Nice desk!"

Angel's brow furrowed slightly at the curious remark, and she turned to see what she was talking about. Her jaw dropped at the sight of the gorgeous walnut slab-top desk sitting where the plywood and crate desk had been. She stepped over to it and carefully put a hand on the rich, glassy surface.

"That's naturally fallen spalted black walnut."

Angel turned to see Chris in the doorway. She looked back at the desk. "It's beautiful." She turned back to look at Chris. "Why?"

Chris looked down at the floor. "Because I'm so sorry."

"For lying to me?"

"Yes."

"For playing me for a fool so Mike could humiliate me at my business in front of a crowd of people including my staff."

Chris slumped. "Yes. I'm very sorry for that."

Angel nodded and stuck her chin out. "Is that all you have to say?"

Chris took a big breath. "I'll add that to forgive is to set a prisoner free and discover that the prisoner was you."

Angel was silent for a moment, then yelled, "What the fuck does that mean?"

Chris flinched. "Well, I think it means that if you can forgive somebody then you—"

"Did you look up that little quotable on your phone just now?"

"Um…Yes."

Angel crossed her arms over her chest. "So, what the hell do you know about what it takes to god damned forgive somebody?"

Chris opened her mouth to say something, but no words came out. Angel watched as the expression on her face went from confusion and panic to sudden realization. And then she spun out of the room.

Angel followed as she ran through the kitchen, plowed past Jo and another staff person as they got ready to carry the wedding cake up the stairs, and pounded her way up the stairway to the rooftop.

Angel was a second behind as Chris threw the door open and rushed across the roof, only stumbling a couple of times on the shaky heels.

Beyond the tables and chairs already set for dinner, Angel could see Mike, Maddie, Lucy, and Ms. Bentley standing under the pergola. Maddie was a vision with the setting sun shimmering off her satin dress. Mike was looking a little sick and like he might sweat through his tuxedo.

Bentley was amplified with a small mic clipped to her collar. "Ladies and gentlemen, friends and family, welcome and thank you for being here on this important day. We are gathered here to celebrate the very special love between Maddie Kemp and Mike Lundgren, by joining them today in matrimony. All of us need and desire to love—"

Bentley paused for a moment while Chris rushed up the side aisle to stop and stand at Mike's side. Mike was no longer looking sick and instead was grinning ear to ear. Chris smiled back at him. Lucy grinned and reached across the aisle to hand her the bride's ring.

Angel slowly walked through the tables and chairs to the back of the seated crowd to watch. She grabbed an empty chair and sat down.

"All of us need and desire to love and be loved," continued Bentley. "To quote Supreme Court Justice Anthony Kennedy, 'No union is more profound than marriage, for it embodies the highest ideals of love, fidelity, devotion, sacrifice, and family. And in forming a marital union, two people become something greater than once they were.'"

Maddie and Mike looked at each other and smiled.

"For some couples, the journey to marriage is easy, and for some the journey is more difficult. From the invitations, the dis-invitations, and the re-invitations, I'm sure you all have gathered that for Mike and Maddie it was more difficult than most. But they've made it, and they should be very proud and happy about that."

A tear rolled out of Mike's eye and down his cheek as he gazed at Maddie.

"But I want them to know that marriage isn't the end of this adventure. It's just another milestone along the way in your relationship. There will be plenty of stretches where your lives together will be smooth sailing and others where the seas will be stormy. Some of those storms may throw you completely off track. Sometimes it will be your own mistakes that send you in the wrong direction. But as long as you commit to try and you work hard, you will get back on that journey together. And it will be worth it in the end, I promise you."

Bentley turned to the crowd.

"If there is anyone here who objects to this marriage, speak now or forever hold your peace."

Even from the back of the crowd, Angel could see the beads of fresh sweat begin to appear on Mike's brow, but there was only silence.

"Michael Lundgren, please say your vows."

Mike nodded and reached in his inside breast pocket. He pulled out a sheet of paper covered in handwriting and looked at it.

"Uh, that's page two," he told Bentley.

He reached into the pocket again and pulled out another sheet.

He smiled and unfolded the paper with shaking hands. "Here's page one." He squinted at the paper. "Oh no! The ink got wet from sweat and I...I think I can still read it." Mike cleared his throat. "I, Michael Peter Lundgren, say to thee, Madilyn Ann Kemp, that I will...um, I can't quite read this part."

Bentley took the papers out of his hands and gave them a little shake to get the wetness off before folding them up in her hand. "Just say what's in your heart, Mike."

Mike looked at Maddie and reached for her hands. "Maddie, I love you." He started to cry. "I want to spend the rest of my life with you. And maybe that will be another fifty years and maybe it will just be till tomorrow." He started to cry harder. "But I don't want to spend any of that time without you." He finished up in a full sob.

"What do you promise, Mike?" Bentley asked gently.

Mike took a couple of deep breaths. "I promise...I *promise* to always try to be the best man I can be for you. Sometimes I might fail, and I hope you will forgive me when I do, but I will always try. Rich, poor, healthy, sick, young, or old, all that stuff, I will always take care of you, Madilyn Ann Kemp, and protect you. And your hopes and dreams and happiness will be mine, too." He started to cry again. "They already are!"

"Maddie, what do you promise Mike?"

"I, Madilyn Ann Kemp, promise to you, Michael Peter Lundgren..." Mike started sobbing. "...to be the best person I can be for you, too. And to support you, and care for you, and protect you, and to love you for the rest of my life."

Angel glanced at Chris and saw that Chris was watching her, too. Angel gave a little smile which Chris returned.

"The rings," said Bentley.

Maddie turned to Lucy, who handed her the gold wedding band. Maddie turned back to Mike, who already had his left hand extended, and she put it on. "I take you, Michael Peter Lundgren, to be my lawfully wedded husband."

Mike turned to Chris. Chris grinned at him and nodded and handed him the ring. He returned the grin and then turned back to Maddie. He put the ring on her extended left hand.

"And I take you, Madilyn Ann Kemp, to be my lawfully wedded wife."

"Now, hold hands and turn to face the crowd," Bentley told the two and they did.

"I introduce to you Mike and Maddie Lundgren."

The crowd cheered.

"You may kiss the bride!"

Mike and Maddie put their arms around each other and kissed. The crowd cheered harder. Then Maddie turned to Lucy and they gave each other a hug. Mike turned to Chris, who held out her arms to him. Angel smiled as she saw Mike give Chris the biggest bear hug she had ever seen a person get in her life.

* * *

Angel, in her chef's apparel, sat on a pedestrian bench outside the restaurant. The sun had gone down, but there was still a purple glow in the western sky over the campus. A full moon was rising over the illuminated capitol dome to the east. School was out, but there were still plenty of college kids roaming up and down the street along with the tourists and regular crowd checking out the little shops and restaurants. A street musician performed on the corner in front of an open guitar case. The summer air was warm and damp and carried the smells of dishes from the restaurants up and down the street.

Angel heard the restaurant door open. She turned to see Elizabeth Bentley in the doorway. Bentley walked over to her.

"Your staff said you were out here taking a break. Mind if I join you?"

Angel shook her head. Bentley sat down on the bench next to her.

They sat in silence, watching the young people stroll up and down the street, some of them hand in hand.

Angel looked down at her hands in her lap. "During the ceremony, when you talked about two people in marriage becoming something greater than they once were…"

"Yes?"

"I was wondering, when, for whatever reason, that greater thing is ripped apart…" Angel choked. She took a breath and continued, "…do you think the person left behind, do you think that person can ever be whole again?"

Bentley took a big breath. "My dear, when a love that strong is created it can never be destroyed. It's made its mark on the universe with pictures, stories, memories, and sometimes children. And if two people can't be together, for whatever reason, I think, yes, the person left behind can still go on to create another love, another thing greater than herself."

Bentley reached over to grasp Angel's hands in her lap. She looked up at her.

"She just has to choose to."

Angel looked at the hands clasped in her lap. She pulled one free to wipe some tears from her face with her sleeve and shrugged.

"What's stopping you?" asked Bentley gently.

Angel took a breath. "If you love somebody, you risk getting hurt very, very badly."

"Yes. You do."

"I can't…I don't…" Angel looked up at her. "It's scary."

"Then be brave."

"I wish I could be fearless, but I'm so afraid—"

"Any idiot who doesn't know what they are getting into can be fearless. A three-year-old with a loaded gun is fearless. Having courage is being afraid and acting anyway." She reached out to lift Angel's chin. "You can do it."

CHAPTER TWENTY-ONE

Chris polished off a second piece of wedding cake while Mike was still working on his first. Normally, he'd be the first person to finish his plate, but he hadn't really stopped talking since the speeches ended and dinner began. He had jabbered through the amuse-bouche, the salad, and the entree. He was quiet for a minute while he and Maddie cut the cake, but as soon as he sat down he was chattering happily again in Chris's ear.

At nine p.m. Olivia's staff began clearing the tables and removing the chairs that had been set up for the ceremony in order to create the dance floor. Chris leaned back in her chair in relief as Bentley came to the head table to congratulate the couple, and she became the focus of Mike's attention instead of Chris. Bentley pointed to the side of the table away from Chris. "Mike, tell these people the story you told me about how you met Maddie."

Mike's face lit up. He turned his back to Chris, leaned in toward the other side of the table, and started the story. Chris knew it very well; she had been the one to introduce them.

Bentley stepped around behind Chris and leaned in close. "Have you talked to Ms. Lux since the ceremony ended?"

Chris peered toward the door to the kitchen stairway. "No. She's been busy in the kitchen, I suppose."

"Well, the kitchen should be winding down. Why don't you go find her while I sit in your chair and have a chat with the happy couple."

Bentley shooed Chris off her chair. She stood awkwardly behind her for a moment, unsure of what to do. Mike turned back around and saw Bentley in her chair and immediately the Englishwoman had him absorbed in an engaging conversation.

Chris turned and slowly walked toward the kitchen stairway, where staff would randomly appear at the door as they cleared plates and drinks and other items. When the coast seemed clear, she opened the door and peered down the stairway. She took a few steps down and peeked into the kitchen where Angel was working next to Jo, cleaning up a workstation.

The activity in the kitchen had died down; a couple of the staff were already discussing a time for their smoke break. Jo spied Chris in the stairway and leaned over to stick an elbow in Angel's side. Angel turned to Jo as she nodded in Chris's direction.

Chris had the urge to rush back up the stairs before Angel got angry at another intrusion in her kitchen, but she glanced at Chris on the stairway, turned and said something to Jo, tossed the dishrag she was using in a bin, and gestured to Chris to come over. She climbed down the rest of the stairs and followed her to the office. Once inside, Angel closed the door.

Chris dug at the floor with the toe of her sandal. "So, I'm not sure how we left it, but I was wondering if you had given any thought to…um…" She glanced up at Angel, "…forgiving me?"

"Yeah, let's see, you had apologized for some stuff, but I don't think you were done."

Chris slouched.

"You want to be forgiven for lying to me and telling me you were straight when you're not."

Chris nodded, looking at the floor. "That would be one more thing."

"And for telling me you were engaged when you weren't."

"That would be another."

"And for pretending that you wanted to kiss me."

"Um…no, that was always…I always wanted to kiss you." Chris looked back up at Angel, trying to read her poker face.

Angel pulled off her cap and ran a hand through her short curls. "I guess I should have known you were a lesbian when I saw your car." She glanced at Chris, a smile tugging at one corner of her mouth.

She gave a little smile back. "Yeah, my car should have been a dead giveaway."

Angel pointed to the desk across the room. "Thank you for the desk, by the way."

Chris grinned. "Do you like it?"

"I love it."

Chris stepped up to the desk and put her hand on the glass-like top. She pulled a drawer out of the desk and held it up to show Angel, pointing at the corner. "All of the joins are dovetailed." She carefully replaced the drawer in the desk and opened and closed a couple more. "You have a drawer here, and another one here, and down here." She turned her back to Angel and bent down low over the desk to point to the desk feet. "Those are brushed stainless steel. They will never rust." She snapped back up and turned to face Angel. "Do you like that?"

Angel quickly averted her eyes and blushed. "Um…yeah, I really love that."

"Good. I wanted you to have it. You know, since we…we broke your last one."

"This one won't break?"

"Oh, no." Chris pushed down hard on the desktop, putting all of her weight into it to demonstrate the lack of give. "You could stand your whole crew on this desk and it wouldn't give an inch. Heavy, though. Oh my gosh, I thought Jo was going to have a heart attack when we carried it in here."

"Hmm." Angel nodded, still by the door, and moved her hand back down to the door handle. "Well, before I put my entire staff on the desk maybe just you and I should test it out first."

Angel threw the lock on the door. Chris smiled.

Angel took a couple of steps closer. Suddenly, desire was thick in the room between them. Chris's heart began to thump, and her breathing quickened. But as Angel got closer, surprise tears filled her eyes and spilled over to run down her cheeks. Looking concerned, Angel lifted her hands to wipe the tears off.

Chris tucked her chin down, embarrassed at the sudden tears and overwhelming emotions she was feeling. "I am so sorry for lying to you. I should have at least told you at dinner at your place. I should have trusted you. I've been terrible—"

"No. I've been the terrible one. I crushed Maddie when I put her wedding into a tailspin. I'm responsible for breaking up your relationship with your best friend. I even put your business in jeopardy. And Mike..." Angel groaned. "Poor Mike. I've really put him through the wringer."

Chris looked up to see tears starting to well in Angel's eyes.

"I've been treating the women in my life very badly the last few years," Angel continued. A tear slipped down her cheek, and then another. "I never had sex with anyone who was completely drunk, but I never approached women who were exactly sober, either." She shook her head and made a noise of disgust. "I don't want to be that person anymore. I want to be somebody better." She drew her forearm up to swipe the tears off her face with her sleeve and then reached forward to thumb the tears from Chris's cheeks. "And braver. I'm going to be braver." Angel took a deep breath and gripped Chris's face between her palms to look her square in the eyes. "I love you, Chris."

Chris felt her heart burst. And the tears that were trickling out before started to pour. "I love you, too."

Angel wrapped her arms around her, and they kissed passionately. Angel pressed herself into Chris and Chris ended up leaning into the desk behind her. Both paused for a moment to look down at the desk, remembering it was there. Chris reached down and stripped her dress off over her head, throwing it on the floor. Angel started to undo the buttons on her chef's coat while Chris reached down to undo the button and zipper on Angel's pants. Soon Angel's clothes were in a pile on the floor next to hers. They shimmied out of their underclothes and in mere seconds were naked on top of the desk together.

Angel kissed her neck and an irrepressible groan escaped Chris's throat. She slapped a hand over her mouth and looked at Angel. "I don't know if…You make me so…" Chris blushed. "I don't know if I can be quiet."

Angel grinned. "I closed the dining room early and sent the staff up to the party. It's okay if you can't be quiet."

Chris smiled and nodded. She rolled over on top and leaned in to kiss Angel's ear and then her neck. Angel took Chris's hand and placed it between her legs. "I need you to touch me."

Chris kissed her mouth and carefully pressed her finger into her center, feeling the heat and wetness and the growing excitement there.

Angel closed her eyes and moaned in pleasure.

Chris began to rhythmically move her fingers, watching the sexual tension build on Angel's face.

"I love you," said Chris.

Angel slightly opened her eyes, her gaze smoky with passion. She reached forward to put her hands on Chris's face. "I love you, too." She kissed her and moaned into her mouth as she climaxed. She collapsed back down onto the desk while Chris kissed her throat and behind her ear. Angel took a moment to catch her breath and then rolled on top of her.

Chris looked up at Angel. "Do the same thing to me."

* * *

Angel and Chris walked together up the stairway from the kitchen where they could hear the music being pumped onto the rooftop by the deejay. As they got to the top Angel paused with her hand on the door. She reached up and smoothed out some of Chris's disheveled honey waves and kissed her firmly.

"We're just going to slip out onto the roof quietly. Hopefully nobody noticed we were gone," she said in a low voice.

"And we'll pretend like I didn't just get my mind blown by some incredible orgasms in your office."

Angel smiled and waggled her eyebrows at Chris, the curl in her right brow flying free. "Exactly."

Angel straightened her shoulders, opened the door and they stepped out onto the rooftop. As soon as they came onto the deck, one whole area of the rooftop turned to them, lifted their drinks, and cheered. The group included Mike and Maddie, Lucy, Jo and a bunch of other crew members from the kitchen, and even a CPA in town that Angel recognized as Linda Pawlowski.

Confused, Angel looked to Chris. She was standing with her hand over her mouth and her eyes open wide in apparent shock as she stared at a large, metal box at the center of the group. The size of a household dishwasher, it was embedded in the roof. Chris had referred to it as an air handling something or other when she was building the patio. The group began to drift away from the box, several of them lifting their glasses to Chris and Angel as they passed.

Angel looked at Chris again, noticing that behind her hand Chris's face had turned beet-red. "What is it? What's going on?"

"Way to go, Chris! Yeah!" yelled Mike, his drink in the air.

Chris nodded and waved at him with one hand while the other remained over her eyes.

"The ventilation system," Chris told Angel.

"What? That big metal thing?"

"The kitchen vents over there," Chris said, pointing to a second big metal thing hidden behind a planter. "The rest of the building vents there." Chris pointed at the first big metal thing.

"Woo-hoo!" yelled Mike as Maddie took him by the hand and dragged him away from the vent.

Chris continued, "The last stop for that system is just below the vent. The office."

"Uh-oh." Angel started to comprehend. "Do you think they could...hear?"

Angel looked back at the vent. Jo gave her two big thumbs-up. Angel looked back to Chris. Chris, her face still behind her hand, nodded.

Angel gritted her teeth. "God dammit!"

Elizabeth Bentley stepped between the two of them.

"No worries, you two!" She pulled Chris's hand off her face and put an arm around each of them. "Grandma Lundgren and the other old people were moved to the other side of the patio. They didn't notice anything. Some of your friends…" Bentley took her arm off Angel and made a so-so motion with her hand. "Say, look! Your chef showed up." Bentley pointed over to Jasper, who was partly leaning on Lucy but smiling through a very puffy face.

Bentley wrapped her arm around Angel again. "Since it appears you two managed to…work things out, shall we say, I'd like to recommend you take a vacation together."

"A vacation?" asked Angel.

"Yes. Just the two of you. And right away. Tomorrow even. Do you have the time?"

Chris and Angel looked at each other.

Chris shrugged. "Mike is going on his honeymoon after the wedding, so I had already scheduled some time off. I don't have any other plans."

Angel nodded. "As long as Jasper is feeling better, he can always run the restaurant without me."

"Where should we go? Too late to book a flight. We'd have to drive."

"Milwaukee? Minneapolis? There's a lot to do in Chicago."

"We could see a play and go to the museums."

"Yeah. The botanical garden in Chicago is beautiful. Maybe a ballgame?"

Bentley shook her head. "No, no. You two could use some quiet time to focus on each other. Away from any distractions. Just the two of you. No work. No responsibilities—"

"I got a puppy."

Angel did a double take at Chris. "A puppy?"

"Do you like puppies?"

Angel grinned. "I love puppies."

Bentley nodded. "The puppy can go along."

Angel cocked her head at Bentley. "Did you have some place in mind?"

Bentley leaned in conspiratorially. "I know the perfect place! It's an adorable bed-and-breakfast just a few hours north in Door County. Beautiful! Quiet. Secluded. Rustic. The menu and buildings could use some work. And if you two leave tomorrow I can get you a free room for a week."

"Really?" exclaimed Chris.

Angel laughed. "Sounds like it was meant to be."

Just then Angel saw a young woman peek around the customer entrance to the patio. Under her arm she was carrying what at first Angel thought was a stuffed animal. When it wiggled, she realized it was a fluffy brown puppy. She carefully stepped inside with it.

Chris looked in the direction of Angel's gaze and waved the woman over. "That's my dogsitter. Is the rooftop pet friendly?"

"Olivia always loved dogs."

The dogsitter walked over to them. "I had an issue come up at my other job. I tried to text, but you weren't answering your phone." She handed Chris the leash. "Okay if I—?"

"Sure." Chris took the leash. "No problem."

Angel took the puppy and was rewarded with a face full of slobbery puppy kisses.

Bentley grinned at Angel and Chris. "You three are adorable. Text me for details regarding the B&B. I'll let the owners know you are coming. I have to stop up there for business, so we will probably see each other again." She gestured at the patio. "Great space, by the way." She winked at Angel. "I'll keep Olivia's in mind for future events." With that she turned and strode away.

Angel and Chris sat down at an empty table with Bear. The deejay started to play a bouncy pop song. Mike got up to dance with Maddie. Lucy danced with Jasper. And Jo invited the CPA, Linda, to the floor.

Angel put her arm around Chris, and Chris leaned into her shoulder. "Do you think Olivia would have liked this? Weddings on the rooftop of her dream restaurant?"

Angel smiled and kissed Chris's hair. "She would have loved it." Angel leaned her head on Chris's. "You know what she would have loved more?"

Chris turned to look up at Angel. "What?"

Angel grinned. "Dancing here." She stood up, took Chris's hand, and pulled Chris and Bear onto the dance floor, where they danced together with old friends and new, joyfully.

Bella Books, Inc.

Women. Books. Even Better Together.

P.O. Box 10543
Tallahassee, FL 32302

Phone: 800-729-4992
www.bellabooks.com